Chances

Ruth Saberton

Edition 1 CSP

Copyright © 2017 Ruth Saberton

All rights reserved.

Title ID: **6897473**
ISBN-13: **978-1542828376**

All characters, organisations and events in this publication, other than those
clearly in the public domain, are fictitious and any resemblance to real
persons, living or dead, is purely coincidental.
The opinions expressed in this book are solely the opinions of the author
and do not represent the opinions or thoughts of the publisher. The author
has represented and warranted full ownership and / or legal right to publish
all materials in this book.
Copyright © 2017 Ruth Saberton
Cover illustration 2017 Dar Albert
The moral right of the author has been asserted.

Notting Hill Press 2017
All rights reserved. No part of this publication may be reproduced, stored
in a retrieval system or transmitted, in any form or by any means, without
the prior permission of the publisher.

A NOTE FROM THE AUTHOR

Dear reader,

Thank you so much for reading CHANCES. I really hope you enjoyed the book. Horses are a huge passion of mine and it's always been a cherished dream to write a pony book. Like Amber, I grew up dreaming about having a horse of my own and lived for my riding lessons or time spent at the stables. That's where any similarities end, though. Amber's road certainly contains a great more obstacles than my own.

Before writing full time I was a teacher, a Head of Year and I also worked as part of a Child Protection team in a big secondary school. I draw upon a lot of my experiences of working with young people for this book and, although CHANCES is 100% fiction and very much in the pony story genre, I hope there's truth here for readers of all ages, backgrounds and interests. Themes such as isolation, illness, misunderstandings, bullying, friendship, parents and children, being a young carer, responsibility and belonging run through the book alongside those of hope, trust and dreams coming true.

This is a novel which means a great deal to me. There are more adventures waiting for Amber, Harry and Drake and if enough readers enjoy CHANCES then I hope to write a sequel. I'm also aiming to donate a percentage of any profits the book makes to equine charities working with young people like Amber in this story.

Reviews are like gold dust and if you could take a moment and pop a review If any reviews could be posted onto Amazon UK or Amazon.com I would be really grateful.

Thanks again, and I really hope you enjoyed the book.

x Ruth x

Ruth Saberton

CHAPTER 1

I knew today was going to be a bad day, not that I needed psychic skills to figure this out. When a social worker, two policemen and a doctor turn up on your doorstep before 8 am it's not usually good news.

But even I didn't think things were going to get this bad.

Here are two things I've learned about social workers:

Number one: they're hardly social – mine never pops round unless she's bringing some message of doom – and number two: which follows on from number one really, they don't seem to do a lot of work. I mean, drinking tea, looking caring and asking me if I'm all right hardly counts as work, does it? Doing two paper rounds before school and long weekend shifts washing up in a café is what I call work. Or rather that's what I did call work because I won't have a job now I've been dragged away without even being consulted, will I? But why should my opinion count? I'm just the one being taken into care. Who cares what I think?

It's only my life.

"Look, Amber, there's no point sitting there glowering. Why don't you try to see this as a wonderful opportunity?"

That's Mrs. Dogood, my social worker, lobbing a few pearls of wisdom at me as she drives along the motorway.

OK, you've got me. Mrs. Dogood isn't her real name. It's Allgood or Bigood or something but I've called her Dogood in my head for years and I think it suits her much better because 'doing good' is exactly what she thinks she's up to. Every time she yanks me away to some new foster placement or core group meeting she thinks she's doing me a favour, the poor deluded woman. She's at it again right now as she witters on about how wonderful it will be for me to have a change of scene and (another) fresh start. If she doesn't shut up soon I think I'll just open the car door and hurl myself under the next passing juggernaut. As if being forced to leave my entire life is wonderful? How she ever got this job is utterly beyond me because the woman hasn't a clue. She actually thinks I should be grateful.

Like, hello? What planet is she on?

Dogood sighs when I don't reply. Even her frizzy hair looks exasperated.

"Why don't you try to look on the bright side?"

I stare at her in disbelief. And what bright side would that be, exactly? The one where I have to leave everything behind? Or maybe the one where I get dumped in the middle of nowhere with yet another load of losers? Call me picky put I'm struggling to see anything vaguely resembling a bright side.

"Cornwall's a beautiful county with wonderful beaches. I bet you'll have a lovely time," Dogood continues in the bright tone of voice you'd use with a six year-old. How she's ended up working with teenagers is a total mystery; she hasn't a clue what makes us tick.

"I don't want to go to the beach," I mutter. "I want to go back to Bristol."

Dogood sighs again. "We've been through this already. There aren't any long-term foster placements in Bristol. This out of county one is all we've got for you at such short notice."

"Why can't I just stay at home?"

This makes total sense to me and I could visit Mum as well as look after Scally, our dog. I bet this would save money too. Since everyone's always banging on about budgets and cuts surely this would make Social Services happy?

Simples.

"You can't stay at home because you're fifteen," my social worker snaps, veering across two lanes of traffic and causing several drivers to gesture and hoot at us. "And before you ask again, the dog will be fine. Your neighbour said she'd feed and walk her."

"But she'll miss me," I whisper. "She's used to seeing me all the time."

When I think of Scally, a mad bouncing ball of scruffy mongrel, sitting by the door waiting and waiting for me to come home, my throat starts to feel all tight and my eyes tingle. To distract myself I pull out my earring and dig the sharp hook into my arm. There's no way I'm going to cry. Absolutely no way.

I'll probably flood the car.

"If I stayed at home you could come and visit me every day to check I'm OK."

I'm clutching at straws now, which is hardly surprising seeing as each mile is taking me further and further west and further and further away from my life. Stuff straws, I'll clutch anything. "I'll go to school. I promise."

"You know as well as I do it doesn't work like that," Dogood says wearily.

Actually I do. I'm quite the expert on foster placements. I'm also an expert on getting kicked out of them. Something tells me I won't be hanging around in Cornwall for too long. Dogood ought to save herself a trip and turn around now. I give it a week, tops, before the latest foster parents are on the phone begging her to come and get me.

"Anyway," she adds thoughtfully, "I think a fresh start is exactly what you need. Let's be honest, things aren't going very well at school are they?"

I glance out of the window at the blur of green hedges. Not going very well is a bit of an understatement. Before social services swooped I was minding my own business on a five-day exclusion, happy to hang out with Jeremy Kyle and the Loose Women while the Education Welfare Officer talked to Mum through the letterbox.

"It's not my fault the teachers hate me."

Yet another sigh. "You don't help yourself, Amber. All they see is a bad attitude. They don't know your case history like we do and it was your decision we didn't tell them, remember? I still think it might have made things easier for you if we had."

I stare down at my bitten nails. There you go, yet more proof she hasn't a clue. The last thing I want is pity. The thought of teachers making allowances because of…

Well anyway, there are just some things that ought to stay private, aren't there? I can't bear the thought of them all gossiping about me in the staff room. I'd rather they just thought I was a stroppy cow.

"And that nose piercing doesn't do you any favours either. It's not part of the uniform code."

"I know," I mutter. "That's why I got it."

"And it's such a shame you dyed your hair!" Dogood shakes her head sadly.

"No wonder they put you out for five days."

I pull down the sun visor and glance in the vanity mirror. A white face floats back at me, green eyes ringed with thick eyeliner and framed by inky black hair. It's not a bad look, a bit Twilighty maybe which is so not my thing, but it certainly made my Head of Year freak which is my thing.

"You've got such beautiful hair," Dogood sighs. "And all those lovely red curls! I can't think what you dyed it for. It really made you stand out."

I roll my eyes at my reflection. Who wants to stand out for being ginger? It's bad enough being lanky and skinny and from the Shakespeare Estate. The last thing I want is to stand out. At my school standing out is a sure way of getting a good kicking.

"I think new start in a new school's just what you need," Dogood tells me brightly. "Your grades have really slipped too, which is such a shame.

You used to be a straight A student, Amber. I don't know what's happened."

"Yes you do," I say under my breath. Of course she knows. It's all there in my case notes.

"You've got your GCSEs in the summer so you need to knuckle down. Living in the country with no distractions is exactly what you need. You'll be glad of this move when you get your results! You'll never be a vet unless you get good exam passes."

The last thing I need is yet another lecture about my (lack of) academic success. I know my grades are bad. I'm the one constantly being nagged about my lack of homework and unfinished assignments, aren't I? And staying away from school to keep an eye on Mum doesn't exactly help improve things, not that I'm going to share this choice detail with Dogood. She'll be typing it up and calling a case conference before you can say at risk.

It's easier just to forget about my GCSEs. I'd probably have been a rubbish vet anyway. I'm rubbish at everything else.

We drive on for what feels like hours and with every mile that takes me further away from Bristol I feel worse. When the car crosses a bridge over a vast river and Dogood declares ecstatically that we're in Cornwall I want to throttle her with her tasseled scarf. What's to be so excited about? How can a glimpse of sea and a few place names written in Cornish thrill her so much?

She needs to get out more. Seriously.

"This is it! St. Perran!" Dogood announces twenty minutes later, slowing the car as we drop down into a valley where houses cling for dear life to the hillside. The sea glitters in the sunshine and a couple of guys with surfboards tucked under their arms stand chatting outside a tiny shop.

A shop? You have to be kidding. This place only has one shop? What on earth do people do here?

"Surf?" suggests Dogood brightly when I voice this thought. "Study? Stay out of trouble?"

Oh God. Kill me now, please, before I die of boredom. Oh look! There goes a piece of tumbleweed.

OK. I may have made that up but you get the gist.

This place is dead with a capital D.

Our car passes through the village and past a long slice of golden beach. Scally would love that beach, but I'm not going to let myself think about Scally right now. Besides, I'll see her very soon. It's not as though I'll be sticking around. We turn left by a church and the road begins to wind out of the village. Dogood chats away about the beautiful countryside but I can't speak. It's all right for her. She's not the one about to be dumped with a load of strangers. I feel as though piranhas are gnawing on my guts. I suppose ought to be used to this but it never gets any easier.

"Nearly there," Dogood trills, turning off the main road. "Oh look! What a lovely house. I wonder who lives there?"

Set back from the lane is a ginormous house, the kind that you'd imagine Cheryl Cole or maybe Wayne Rooney living in, if they'd ever be daft enough to move this far from civilization of course. I'm not very interested in houses, unlike my mum who on her good days loves watching property shows and pretending she can afford to buy one. She's got a good imagination I'll say that for her because some days we can't even afford a can of baked beans.

No, what catches my eye are the fields surrounding the house, bowling green smooth and fringed with post and rail fencing. These paddocks are filled with horses grazing contentedly and they aren't any old horses either. I haven't ridden for years, not since Dad left, but I know quality horses when I see them. As we drive by I watch a stunning grey, ridden by a blonde girl, floating around an arena while a dark haired boy leans against the fence and looks on devotedly.

There you go. Some people really do have it all. I must have done really something bad in a past life.

"Oh look! We're here!" Dogood says delightedly, slowing to pass through tatty gate with the name Perranview Farm nailed onto it. The car bounces along a drive full of potholes and moments later we pull up outside a farmhouse which has definitely seen better days. Ivy smothers the walls, paint peels from the window frames and the yard is little more than a patch of mud.

And they were worried about leaving me on the Shakespeare Estate?

Dogood yanks up the hand brake and smiles at me.

"Are you ready to say hello? Please make an effort, this placement could be really good for you."

I don't reply. What's the point?

I'm far too busy planning what I can do to get sent home.

CHAPTER 2

"Have some fruit cake, Amber. I only made it this morning and if you don't grab a slice quickly the rest of my gannets will gobble the lot!"

Kate Crewe, my latest foster mother, smiles at me but I don't smile back. Does she really think I'm going to be won over by a slice of cake? In her dreams. She might have gathered everyone around the enormous farmhouse table and practically drowned us with cups of tea but it takes more than this to make me play happy families. Anyway, I've got my own family back in Bristol; Mum, Scally and me. We might not be happy exactly but we're OK. Or at least we were until I got dragged here.

"It looks lovely," gushes Dogood, helping herself to a huge slice. "Doesn't it, Amber?"

"No," I say, wrinkling my nose in what teachers always tell me is a really unattractive sneer. "I think it looks gross."

Everyone stares at me - Kate, her two children, Dogood, several dogs and three cats - and they all look shocked. I'd say that's a strike. A few more days acting up like this and I'll soon be packed off home. It's easy when you know how.

"Don't you like cake?" This question comes from Kate's daughter, Maddy, who's sitting next to me. I've only been here ten minutes and already she's driving me mad by following me around and asking about a million questions. If I stay here too long my mum won't be the only one who needs a shrink.

"I hate cake." I curl my lip. "It makes you fat, doesn't it?"

Kate looks taken aback. A plump woman in her forties, she's obviously more than partial to a slice or six of cake.

"Err, right. Maybe a biscuit then?"

I ignore her and yawn rudely, giving everyone a view of my tongue stud. Bet they love that.

"Amber!" hisses Dogood. "What's got into you?"

"Not cake, that's for sure," observes the boy sitting opposite. Blue eyes beneath a shock of thick blonde hair narrow at me as he leans across the table and helps himself to a slice. "It's your loss. This is great as always, Mum."

Kate beams at him. "Harry's always hungry. It's working on the farm, isn't it love? Gives you such an appetite."

Harry can't speak, his mouth is too full, but his freckled face dimples at his mother in reply and I look away. Vomit making shows of family affection are a bit more than I can stand right now.

"There must be lots to do on the farm," says Dogood, hastily changing the subject. "Amber loves animals. Maybe she can lend a hand?"

Kate smiles at me. "I'm a sucker for waifs and strays, I'm afraid, Amber. There are always lambs needing bottle feeding. Once we even had a pet seagull! Harry and Maddy will show you around when you've finished your drink. There's so much to do on a farm. We never seem to stop."

"Am I here because you need somebody to work? I thought child labour was illegal?" I say nastily.

A blush stains Kate's neck. "I just thought if you like animals…"

Her voice tails off and she stares miserably down at the table while Dogood looks daggers at me.

Amber one. Losers nil. This is almost too easy.

There's an uncomfortable silence in the kitchen. Harry's glaring at me and I don't blame him. If anyone talked to my mum like that I'd probably thump them. He's protective of Kate and I totally get it. On the journey down Dogood told me all about how Kate's husband died a couple of years back and that her son had to quit Art College to run the farm. Harry might want to bury his cake fork in my head but we've got more in common than he'll ever know. I've been trying to quit school for ages so I can look after my mum too and make sure she doesn't… doesn't…

Well, never mind all that. I just want to make sure Mum's all right. That's why I give the teachers attitude at school. If I get kicked out then I can stay at home and keep an eye on her. It makes perfect sense.

Something cold presses against my hand and looking down I see a black Staffy looking up at me with big melting Malteaser eyes. I scratch the top of her head and try not to think about Scally all alone in the flat and wondering where I am.

"Look, Mum!" Maddy shrills, making everybody jump. "Saffy Staffy likes Amber! That's amazing!"

Kate follows her daughter's gaze. "Goodness! How unusual! She really does like you, Amber."

I must have made a really bad impression if they're this surprised a dog thinks I'm bearable.

"Amber's good with animals," Dogood says quickly. "She wants to be a vet."

"A vet?" Harry's blonde eyebrows shoot into his fringe. "You must be much more intelligent than you look, Amber."

"Harry!" Kate gives her son a warning frown. To me she says, "Saffy's a rescue dog. She'd been locked in a shed and beaten, I guess they wanted to toughen her up and make her fight, so she finds it hard to trust anyone. It's really unusual for her to approach a stranger."

I glance down at the dog. Her head's resting on my knee now and her eyes are closed. My fingers drift across the silky dome of her head.

"You have a gift," Kate says softly. "She trusts you."

I feel myself start to blush. I might have dyed my hair but I'm still a ginger underneath.

"Come and meet the other animals! See if they like you too!" Maddy shrieks, grabbing my hand and tugging me to my feet. Before I even have a second to refuse or to think of a sarcastic comment she's dragged me out of the kitchen and into the yard where I'm introduced to goats, chickens, cats and a even a snoring pig called Michael.

"He's named after the man who owns our farm," giggles Maddy, leaning into the stall to scratch Michael's prickly back. "Don't tell him. He'll probably kick us out!"

"I thought your mum owned the farm?"

She shakes her head. "We rent it. That's why Harry works so hard. If we can't pay the rent we'll lose it even though our family's lived here forever. Mum doesn't think I know but I've heard them talking. They had a massive row when Harry left college and Mum cried lots."

Mums who cry lots is something I do know about. And so is having to give up things you care about to help them. No wonder Harry's got such a giant chip on his shoulder.

"Harry's a really good artist," Maddy adds proudly. "Maybe he'll sketch you?"

I think this is very unlikely. The way her brother was glowering at me he looked more likely to stab me with a pencil and when operation get sent back really kicks off I don't think he'll feel any differently. Still, Maddy's just a little kid so I humour her.

"Maybe," I nod.

"I really wish my dad hadn't died," says Maddy. "Is your dad dead too?"

I'm taken aback. "What?"

"Your dad? Is he dead?" Maddy asks, quite cheerfully considering the subject matter. "Mine is. A tractor squashed him. What happened to yours?"

That's the million dollar question. Nothing as exciting as getting squashed by a tractor, that's for certain. It was more a case of not being able to handle Mum any more and taking off, not that I'm going to try and explain all this to an eleven year old.

After all, he didn't.

"My dad left," is all I say.

"Like went away? Proper away? Not to Heaven?"

I snort. "There's no way my dad will go to Heaven!"

"So will he come back again and you'll live happily ever after?"

I think of Mum all alone in the hospital, the days when we can't afford to buy much food and the knocks on the front door that send us scuttling to hide behind the sofa. Then I think about being dumped here, miles away from everyone and everything I know and my throat feels all tight and funny.

I think we can safely say I won't be living happily ever after any time soon.

After Michael the pig I'm introduced to Minty the sheep and then Maddy drags me to a paddock overlooking the sea where a Shetland pony regards us beadily from beneath a thick ginger forelock.

"This is Treacle, he's the grumpiest pony in the world," she informs me proudly, waving a tuft of grass in his direction. When Treacle finally bothers to potter over I scratch his neck and talk to him like I used to do to the ponies at the riding school and blow into his nose.

"He likes you too!" Maddy shrieks. "Normally he bites everyone! Mum's right, Amber! You're like Dr. Doolittle!"

"Hardly!" I laugh. It's true though; animals always seem to like me. It's just as well somebody does.

When we return to the farmhouse I'm horrified to discover Dogood's done a runner. It's not that I'm upset she's left without saying goodbye, believe me I really don't care about that, but part of me was still hoping there'd be a reprieve at the eleventh hour and she'd drive me home. Now it looks as though I'm stuck in pasty land for however many days it takes Kate to realize she can't handle me. I'm really annoyed with myself for being distracted by the animals. That was definitely an own goal.

"We'll have supper in a bit," Kate tells me. She's stirring something on the Aga and it smells absolutely delicious. The dogs and cats gathered at her feet stare up hopefully.

"I'm not hungry," I say.

What a fib! I'm famished. There was nothing at home to eat at breakfast, Dogood was so keen to get rid of me that we didn't stop on the journey and then of course there was the cake I refused just to make a point. I think my stomach's forgotten what food is.

"What a shame. I thought you'd be ravenous after your journey and all the fresh air here." Kate gives the pan one last stir and bangs the lid on. "I've made Irish Stew with dumplings. Well, never mind. How about you go and settle into you room and I'll put some aside for you? You may want it later."

"I won't. I hate stew." I screw up my nose for good effect.

Kate looks worried. "You're not a vegetarian are you, Amber? Nobody has mentioned any special diets. Shall I make you something else?"

I shrug. "Don't care. Whatever."

"Do you like omelets? The hens have laid brilliantly today. Or what about some pasta?"

Is she for real?

"Stop it, Mum, she's just being a pain in the butt," says Harry who's leaning against the Aga, all long legs, strong tanned arms and blonde curls falling across his face. When he brushes them back I can see the expression in his eyes and I look away quickly. Wow. It didn't take long to make him hate me. I think that's a record even for Amber Evans.

"Don't Harry," Kate says gently. "Amber's had a tough day."

"Haven't we all?" says Harry icily. Tell you what, Amber, I'll carry your bag up and you can unpack. You never know that might help you work up an appetite."

He scoops up my bag and stomps out of the kitchen, ducking his head to miss the low door frame. Annoyed, I follow him up a twisty staircase and along a corridor leading to a narrow flight of attic stairs. Once at the top he flings the door open to reveal a sunny room with a big bed smothered in a faded patchwork quilt, gingham curtains blowing in the breeze and a huge squashy armchair. There's even a desk with an angle poise lamp should I have a violent personality change and wish to do some homework.

It's a million miles away from the corner of the lounge I have at home.

"You've got the best view up here," Harry remarks as he places my bag on the bed and strides to the window. "You can see for miles."

I follow him and we lean on the wide sill to gaze outside. He's right; the view is like something from one of Mum's favourite property shows, you know - the kind where people with loads of money escape to the country. Wow. Mum would love this view! If I look to the left I can see over Treacle's orchard and right out to sea across endless miles of deep blue water. In the other direction is St. Perran and through the trees I spot the big house I passed earlier and, to my delight, the fields of beautiful horses.

I can see horses from my bedroom!

"Who lives there? Who owns those horses?"

"So she can speak without being insulting?" Harry says. "Amazing."

I give him a look that ought to lay him out at my feet. "Just answer the question."

"I'll answer your questions if you lay off my mum for five minutes, stick a smile on that sulky face of yours and come down and eat some dinner," he says, folding his arms and staring down at me. "It's a fair bargain,

Amber. Don't they say that knowledge is power?"

For a split second I consider telling him to get lost but then I watch a big bay thoroughbred canter across a paddock. Such a stunning horse! Maybe whoever owns it would let me have a look? I know I won't be here for long but even so... you don't see many horses on the Shakespeare Estate, except in the window of the bookies, which isn't quite the same.

"All right," I say grudgingly. "I'll eat a bowl of stew if it makes you happy."

"I couldn't care less what you eat," Harry says cheerfully. "Stay up here and starve yourself if you want; it doesn't bother me. But it will upset Mum and I'm not having that. She works really hard to keep this family together and whatever issues you have, none of them are her fault. She's offering you a home so you could be a bit more grateful."

"I have a home, thanks," I snap. "And grow up, your mum's not a saint. She's getting paid for having me."

He whistles. "Nice attitude! Look, I'm sorry they've taken you into care. It must suck, but that's not Mum's fault. And she's certainly not on a mission to make money out of fostering. Mum could get five times more renting this room out as a bed and breakfast or holiday let. She fosters because she wants to help, and believe me there are loads of kids out there she's really made a difference to. You're nearly sixteen and apparently bright enough to be a vet, so tell me - have you met many millionaire foster parents?"

"Yeah, yeah, whatever." I am so not sticking around for a lecture. "Look, I said I'd eat the dinner, didn't I? So stop going on."

Harry sighs. "Look, Amber, I know this can't be easy but I guess what I'm trying to say is just give us a chance. You never know, you might even like it here."

I think there's more chance of me getting ten starred GCSEs but I decide to keep my mouth shut. Anyway, it's not Harry I need to annoy. This placement's nothing to do with him and if he's constantly on my case things will be twice as complicated.

"So who owns those horses?" I repeat.

"Michael Lacey, our landlord. He owns that big house too and pretty much everything else in St. Perran. He's loaded."

"Pig man?"

Harry laughs and I like the way his eyes crinkle. "Keep that to yourself for God's sake! But yes, pig man! Michael's a big landowner and those horses are his daughter's eventers. Since she moved here her dad certainly spares no expense."

"Is she blonde? I think I saw her riding earlier."

"That's Emily," nods Harry. "She's a nightmare. Totally twists Mike round her little finger and when he's away on business she runs riot. Her parties are legendary in St. Perran. Just about anything goes."

I understand. Our neighbours in Bristol throw similar parties. The only difference is they live in a council flat not a mansion and the police often raid it. Maybe I won't share this detail with Harry, especially since he's so close to Kate. She must have read my case file. Not a happy thought.

"She was with a guy." I recall the gorgeous boy, all smoldering good looks and raven black hair. "Dark hair? Quite tall?"

Harry's face clouds over. "That'll be Drake Owen. He's Emily's trainer."

Drake Owen. That sounds familiar. For a moment I struggle to place him then the name falls right into place. All those sneaky hours in W H Smith spent reading Your Horse magazines I can't afford to buy haven't been wasted; I know exactly who Drake Owen is and excitement zips through me.

Drake Owen is only Britain's hottest and youngest three day event star. He's taken grand slam titles, won Badminton on his eighteenth birthday and is eventing's brightest hope for gold at the next Olympics. Oh, and he's utterly, utterly gorgeous with the brownest eyes, lean fit body and cheekbones steeper than the Hickstead Bank. Add breeches, scarlet cross-country colours and a grin that could melt polar ice caps and there he is: complete perfection.

I may once have stuck a picture of him in my school planner but that's staying top secret.

I'm living next door to Drake Owen? Seriously?

I know I'm not staying here for long but suddenly things are starting to look up.

CHAPTER 3

"That was lovely, mum." Harry slaps yellow butter onto a doorstop of bread, mops up his gravy and munches contentedly. How he's not the size of a house I'll never know because I don't think I've ever seen anyone eat so much. He must have had about three helpings and half a loaf. This farm work he does must be seriously physical.

"Any more for you, Amber?" Kate asks, with the kind of nervous caution you might use creeping up on wildebeest in the Serengeti. The poor woman can hardly believe I've actually eaten my dinner. She daren't spook me now.

"I'm full," I say and then, catching Harry's eye, "thanks."

"You're very welcome, love." Kate scoops up my plate, which to my annoyance I find I've totally cleared. Maybe hunger striking isn't going to work for me? The stew was absolutely delicious and I simply couldn't stop myself from gobbling it up. When I go home I'm going to try and make it for Mum. No more microwave meals for us.

While Kate stacks the dishwasher and chats away and Harry helps himself to a giant slice of apple pie, I look around the kitchen figuring now's as good a time as any to check out my latest prison. There's an ancient Welsh dresser in the corner crammed with junk, rosettes and what look suspiciously like red bills (I'm an expert on those) a massive cream Aga which is like something out of one of Mum's cherished property shows and a tatty sofa leaking stuffing all over the flagstones which seems to be home to all the dogs and cats. There aren't any fitted units, unlike at my last foster placement where Auntie Sue (I kid you not, she made me call her that) spent hours bleaching and polishing every surface and had a fit if I so much as dropped a crumb. Here all the action seems to take place on the battered kitchen table, from eating dinner to Maddy doing her homework to cleaning boots.

Hygienic it is not. Auntie Sue would freak, especially if she saw the cats busily licking piles of plates in the sink. I kind of like it though, or least I like the animals. Everything else still sucks.

"Cup of tea?" Kate asks as she places the kettle on the hot plate. "Or are you a coffee person?"

For a split second I toy with the idea of ignoring her but Harry's beady eyes are still watching my every move and a deal's a deal, isn't it?

"I drink both," I say, "but I'm too full right now. I think I'll go for a walk."

"I'll come! I'll come!" squeaks Maddy, jumping up and down like Tigger. "Let's go to the beach!"

What is it with everyone here and their obsession with beaches? The sea's cold and wet and the sand is scratchy, or at least it was the one time Mum and me went to Weston Super Mare for the day. Besides, I've got better things to do than splash in rock pools with an ankle biter. I want to go and have a look at those horses.

"You've got homework to do," Kate reminds Maddy. To me she says, "Don't go too far, Amber, will you? You don't know your way around yet and the cliffs can be really dangerous if you don't know the tracks."

"Don't panic, I'm not suicidal yet," I say airily.

Kate blanches. So she has read my case notes then.

"Chill out, Mum," says Harry from over the top of Farmers Weekly. "Amber's spotted Mike's horses and she wants to have a look, that's all. She's not going anywhere near the cliffs."

Kate looks relieved. "There's a footpath through the orchard that goes to Michael's place. You can't miss it. I use it when I go cleaning and it's pretty well trodden."

"That's because you do far too much cleaning," laughs Harry but I can tell from the look on his face that he isn't really joking.

"Borrow some wellies if you like, there are loads in the porch and it'll be muddy in the woods," Kate says, looking dubiously at my fake Uggs.

"And watch out for Drake Owen," adds Maddy, glancing up from her school bag. "He might kill you."

My mouth swings open on its hinges. "What?"

"Maddy! That's enough!" says Kate sharply.

"But he might!" protests Maddy. "Harry said —"

"Harry says far too much, and all of it nonsense." Kate's eyes are bright with anger as she rounds on her son. "I've told you before to drop all this. I won't be having it. Do you hear me? Just let it go!"

Now I'm intrigued and not just because they're talking about sex -on -a - stick Drake either. I've been trying to get a reaction out of Kate ever since I arrived and so far nothing from my trusty box of tricks has worked but one mention of Drake Owen and she flies off the handle?

This could be very useful.

Like his mother, Harry is also crimson with anger. "It's not nonsense. For God's sake, Mum! You heard what they said at the inquest. The Owens were to blame! They as good as killed him. They're murderers!"

"I said enough!" Kate's raised voice is enough to silence her son. I must admit I jump too and since I'm a girl who makes teachers holler on an hourly basis this is quite an achievement. "Let it go, Harry, for God's sake. What's done is done."

But the look on Harry's face says quite the opposite and even though I don't give a monkey's about these people – I've learned the hard way there's no point getting attached to foster families – I'm intrigued. Maybe I'll barter a bit more good behaviour with Harry for a few more answers? Anything I find out about Drake Owen has to be interesting, especially if it makes Kate freak out.

Leaving the Crewe family in full squabble I tug on some muddy Hunter wellies that I find in the porch and set off in the direction of Michael Lacey's house. Kate's worn path is easy to follow and as I stomp through the orchard Saffy joins me, barking excitedly and zig -zagging across the track as she investigates all the exciting doggy smells. It's a lovely evening and even though it's autumn the sun is warm and trickles across the path like honey. Scally would love it here. She'd be wagging her stumpy little tail and bringing me sticks to throw. She loves playing fetch.

Oh no. There's a football-sized lump in my throat now. I really hope Scally's all right. I've never been away from her for this long before.

I'm just about to pull my earring out to distract myself from these miserable thoughts when I reach the end of the orchard and a rickety style requires both my hands and quite a lot of balance to clamber over. By the time I've managed to reach the other side without getting my skirt tangled I'm feeling calmer. Calling Saffy to heel I follow Kate's path through a wood until at last I reach the smart post and rail fencing that marks the start of Michael Lacey's paddocks. Sure enough here are the horses I saw from the bedroom window, grazing peacefully in the evening sunshine and swishing away the flies with their long silky tails.

When I was younger, before Dad did a runner, I used to spend every spare minute at the stables. If I wasn't on horseback I was cleaning tack or mucking out in the hope of earning an extra ride. As I watch these beautiful horses, very different creatures from the fat hairy ponies I used to ride, it feels like I've hitched a lift in the Tardis and am being whizzed back in time. I'd forgotten how just being with horses is enough to make everything else fade away. I'd lived for my lessons and especially the times when we were allowed to jump. Nothing beat that amazing adrenalin rush as you gathered up your horse before a fence, judging the stride and feeling the cold wind against your face when you flew into the air. I'd loved every minute but riding costs money and once Dad pushed off Mum and I didn't have a lot of that to spare.

Besides, I didn't like the idea of leaving Mum alone.

I lean against the fence and admire the horses. Although I haven't ridden for ages I've read enough magazines to know that these ones are seriously expensive. Well muscled and sleek, they look every inch pampered athletes and I can just imagine them leaping huge ditches as they gallop across country or perhaps doing a perfect collected canter around the dressage arena. Their tack room must be smothered with rosettes.

Michael Lacey's daughter is one lucky girl.

Gradually the horses notice me and wander over on the off chance I might have some treats. The big grey nudges my pockets hopefully while the small bay thoroughbred stamps his hoof with impatience.

"I haven't got anything," I tell them, as I scratch necks and blow into velvet soft noses. Maybe next time I'll bring some Polos or a crust of bread? Not that there will probably be a next time. With any luck I'll be back home soon.

I'm so busy patting the horses and loving the velvet texture of their clipped coats beneath my fingertips that I almost leap into orbit when there's a thunder of hooves and two riders come cantering along the path. The horses I'm petting spin around and squeal before kicking up their hooves and galloping away with shrill whinnies. Flattening myself against the fence I prepare to be well and truly squashed by the blonde girl bearing down on me at alarming speed.

"Slow down, Emily!" shouts the second rider. "And soften your hands! That gag is on the bottom ring!"

Oh my flipping life. It's Drake Owen. It really, really is and he's even better looking in real life. Forget any member of One Direction or male model types. They'd never look as good in cream breeches, black boots and crimson hoody as Drake does. All those magazine articles haven't done him justice.

Emily yanks her horse to a halt and egg white foam flies through the air. I glance at her hands and shudder. Drake's right, she's holding the reins far too tightly and her fingers are set like concrete. That poor horse.

"What the Hell do you think you're doing?" she demands, glaring down at me with eyes like glaciers. "This is private land and you're trespassing! And get away from my horses!"

Trespassing? I'm a taken aback. Kate doesn't seem the kind to trespass and she's worn a path right to the big house.

"Whatever," I say.

Emily's eyes narrow. "Are you a gypsy?"

I look down at my long tasseled skirt and wellies. Add to this my dyed black hair, thick eyeliner and hooped earrings and I can see where she's coming from. This look works in Bristol but obviously country bumpkins don't get it. Perhaps I should have worn a smock, chewed some straw and said, "Ooo ah"?

"I'm sick of you lot," Emily continues without waiting for my reply. She's way too busy delving into the pocket of her Toggi jacket and pulling out a brand new iPhone to care what I might say. "I'll give you two minutes to get off my land or I'm calling the police."

Wow. I've not even been here twenty-four hours and already the law is being called out on my behalf? Kate will freak and I'll be sent home. Excellent!

I put my hands on my hips. "Go on then. Call them if you want."

"Actually, Emily, she isn't trespassing," Drake Owen says. Reins held loosely in one hand as his horse prances and sidles, he points towards a wooden sign at the entrance of the woods. "This is a public footpath. Anyone can walk along it. Besides, she isn't doing any harm."

Emily's top lip curls. God, I hope I don't look constipated like that when I sneer. Maybe all those teachers had a point after all? It's really not a great look.

"Why are you sticking up for her?"

"Because she hasn't done anything wrong," Drake says calmly. "She's on a public foot path."

"A foot path on my father's land!"

"It's still a public foot path and she's perfectly entitled to use it."

Emily looks from Drake to me and back again. Her eyes glitter with anger.

"Keep away from my horses," she hisses, pointing her whip at me. Then she digs her heels into her mount's flanks and gallops away while I squash myself against the fence and fear for my toes.

Drake Owen exhales wearily and soothes his own horse as it snatches the reins in eagerness to tear after its companion.

"I'm really sorry about that," he says. "Emily can be a fiery but she doesn't mean it. She's all right really."

Aren't men thick where pretty girls are concerned? Emily totally meant it. And as for fiery? Can't say that's my adjective of choice. The one I'd have chosen is cow.

"I was only looking at the horses," I explain, still stunned to be face to face with one of my equestrian idols. "I wasn't feeding them or anything like that. It's just that they're so beautiful…"

My words tail off miserably. Nice one Amber. Who goes around mooning over horses at your age? He must think you're a total sad case.

But to the contrary, Drake treats me to a cute and dimpled grin.

"You're so right, they are beautiful. I could spend hours looking them. See that bay, Monty? He's only just come sound after being lame for six months. Believe me I can't get enough of watching him now! That horse could jump the moon he's got so much heart."

I smile back because the delight in his voice is catching. Just as well Dogood can't see me. She'd pop a blood vessel if she knew Amber Evans could smile.

"He's stunning," I say.

"He is, isn't he?" agrees Drake. "God, that probably sounds terribly boastful but I really do love that horse. He gave me my first ride round Badminton and believe me he did it all. I just clung on and prayed!"

I laugh. "I saw you ride that course and I think you did a bit more than cling on. Didn't you win?"

Beneath his jockey skull Drake blushes. "Err, maybe, but Monty's taught me a lot. Even though he's retired now there's life in him yet."

"He's lovely," I agree and we smile shyly at each other.

"Anyway, I guess I'd better catch up. Sorry again about Emily," Drake says eventually, when we've stopped grinning at each other like idiots. "Enjoy the rest of your walk and feel free to stroke Monty any time you like. And if you pop by again he loves carrots!"

I watch him canter away after Emily, popping the horse effortlessly over the big gate into the woods. Wow. What a rider. And what a gorgeous guy too. It's such a shame he's with that horrible Emily. What on earth does he see in somebody like her? Apart from money, stunning looks and amazing horses of course. I guess some people really do have it all, just like some people really do have nothing.

Even though I don't plan to stay here long I really hope I don't come across Emily Lacey again in a hurry. Something tells me she's the type to hold a grudge.

CHAPTER 4

It might not even be registration time yet but I already know Perran Community Academy and myself are not going to get on and that all Dogood's nonsense about a new start is exactly that: nonsense.

Things are going to be just as bad here as they are at my own school. In fact, forget just as bad; they're going to be even worse. At least back at my own school people give me a wide berth, staff as well as kids, and I know exactly how the system works. Coming from the Shakespeare Estate is a bit like wearing a suit of armour so most kids keep their distance, probably thinking I'm going to set my pit bull on them or something, and when I do attend I generally make it through the day.

Take it from me; surviving school is tough and I've no idea why ITV bothers flying celebrities out to Australia. If they really want to watch Z listers suffer why not drop them into the average British comp? There they can have their eyes taken out by monster rucksacks as they brave the Year Seven corridor stampede, fight to the death for a place in the lunch queue crush and negotiate the shark infested waters of student cliques. Even Bear Grylls would be in tears.

All this before you've even tried to figure out which exam syllabus they use or have sussed out the teachers…

And talking of my new teachers, I didn't even manage to find my way to my form room – predictably sent the wrong way by the person I'd asked – before one of them had a go at me about my lack of blazer. He didn't even let me draw breath to explain I was new or that I have a note but instead handed me a red slip and told me to report to him at lunchtime for a detention. He didn't like it much when I screwed the slip up and threw it on the floor and liked it even less when I walked away mid lecture. And all this before registration too. I'd say that's even a record by my standards. Hopefully I'll be excluded by lunchtime, Kate will admit defeat and I'll be back in Bristol by the weekend.

Now, that's what I'd call a result.

Anyway, this starting a new school business is totally brutal but I know exactly what to expect and it's comforting in a weird kind of a way to not be disappointed. I might be hundreds of miles away from my usual school but some things are depressingly familiar the world over. Teachers always take one look at me with my not quite right uniform, dyed hair and nose stud and label me trouble before I've even made it to my desk. Why should this dump should be any different just because it's in the sticks?

"Have a great day, love," were Kate's parting words when she dropped me at the school gate and it was all I could do not to shoot back a sarcastic reply. Only the agreement I'd struck with Harry kept me quiet but honestly, a great day? Was she for real? I was willing to bet Daniel had a better time stepping into the lions' den than I was about to have at my new school.

It had been weird waking up in the attic bedroom and as the sun poured through the curtains my heavy eyes were gritty from lack of sleep. I'd taken ages to drop off, not because I was nervous but mainly because my brain was busy trying to work out just how soon I could get home again and I felt on edge because the place was just so quiet. When you're used to the rumble of traffic, wail of sirens and yelling neighbours it's weird to hear nothing but hooting owls and the distant sound of waves. It was dark too, a thick blackness that I'd never experienced before and I'd lain staring into the darkness, the duvet pulled up to my chin and jumping out of my skin every time a fox shrieked. When the door creaked open and Saffy padded across the floorboards to press a cold nose into my hand, I cried out. The sound of my own voice was shockingly loud in the silence. Once she leapt onto the bed, though, I began to relax. Used to Scally lying across my legs every night I could almost believe this heavy weight was my own dog and that I was curled up on my sofa bed with Mum fast asleep in her small bedroom.

My mum. I'd really hoped that she was asleep. It wouldn't be quiet where she was, I knew that much. I'd visited her on the wards enough times to have heard the shouting, the clanging doors and…

Anyway. Mum needed me to care for her and I had to get back. Had to. I couldn't get distracted by horses or Drake Owen or any pathetic dreams I might have about riding again. That all belonged to a different life, the one where Dad was still on the scene and there were two of us to worry about Mum. Now it was just me so I couldn't let her down.

I couldn't.

I must have drifted off at this point because the next thing I knew sunshine was streaming in through the gaps in the curtains and Maddy was thumping on my door telling me breakfast was ready.

Breakfast? Seriously? This was a novelty. There's nothing much in our fridge usually, unless you fancy sprouting onions or mold, and on the days I do go to school I tend to just grab a Red Bull and some crisps from the corner shop. I was about to snap that I don't eat breakfast when I remembered my agreement with Harry. I might not be staying but never let it be said Amber Evans goes back on a deal. That kind of rumour gets a girl in big trouble on the Shakespeare Estate. Besides, the smell of bacon was drifting up the stairs and my mouth started to water. As I'd got dressed I'd told myself this was another reason to get home as fast as possible – I'd be the size of a house if I lived here for long.

I ate breakfast in the kitchen with Kate and Maddy, Harry apparently being up and out hours ago doing whatever it is farmers have to do, and then Kate drove us into the next big town in an ancient car held together by dog hair and sweet wrappers. It was further away than I'd imagined and the narrow lanes were a total maze of green but before long Maddy and I were deposited by the school gates and left to fend for ourselves.

Have a great day.

Yeah right.

It could have been worse though, at least Kate didn't insist on accompanying me inside like Auntie Sue would have done. That was a total invitation for every kid to have a go at me and I hadn't even lasted the week before I'd been excluded. I'd not lasted much longer at Auntie Sue's after that either.

Now, there's a thought…

Feeling slightly cheered by at least having something like an escape plan, I was following Maddy to the reception when she grabbed my arm and yanked me into a doorway. Seconds later three blonde girls swished by in a cloud of perfume and superiority, giggling loudly and tossing their hair like show ponies. One of them was Emily Lacey, she of the cast iron hands, gorgeous horses and uber fit boyfriend.

Seeing my astonished expression, Maddy said quickly, "I try and stay away from them. They're not very nice to me because of the farm belonging to Emily's dad and Mum being a cleaner."

I'd been in enough schools to know girls like these weren't very nice to anyone and having already met the charming Emily I totally got why Maddy would avoid her.

"What's she doing at the local comp? If pig man's so loaded, surely she should be at a posh private school?"

"She used to go to boarding school but she's persuaded her dad to send her here," Maddy explained. "She says this way she can be at home and spend more time with the horses but Harry thinks it's really so she can do what she likes while her dad's away."

"Does Pig Man work away much then?"

Maddy nodded. "He goes away lots and lots leaves Emily on her own. Mum says it's neglect."

She clapped her hand over her mouth and stared at me in horror. "I'm not supposed to repeat that in case Mum loses her job."

On the Shakespeare Estate Emily's scenario isn't so unusual and speaking as a girl whose dad went away and totally forgot to come back, I've been pretty much doing what I like for years. The only difference is I don't live in a posh house or have lots of money which means I'm on an at risk list with hot and cold running social workers while girls like Emily get to ride horses and throw parties.

Such is life.

"I won't say anything," I promised and was just on the brink of telling Maddy to let me know if Emily gave her any trouble when I had to stop myself in time. What was I thinking? I couldn't make promises I had no intention of keeping since I was intending to be out of here asap.

It's the golden rule of being on a foster placement: don't get involved.

So, anyway here I am now, clutching a time table that may as well be written in Chinese for all the sense I can make of it, and trying to find my tutor room. This is easier said than done since all these corridors look identical. I'm deep in a maze of blue carpet, flaking ceilings and tatty noticeboards and feeling more lost with each passing second. At regular intervals along the grey walls are cell doors and one of these by a process of elimination has to be my tutor base. Knowing my luck, it'll be room 101.

I glance down at the time table clutched in my hand. No, my tutor base is in K3 which is right in front of me. I suppose this is it. Time to face the lions.

I knock on the door and let myself in without waiting for an answer. Instantly the fug of sweaty teenagers, cheap perfume and board cleaner wallops me. How is it that all schools smell the same? Do they have some special plug in scent that they bulk buy in the same place where they get those blue plastic chairs with the holes in the back and legs that snap off if you swing on them for long enough?

Hostile eyes are instantly trained on me and yes, I'm including the teacher in that too because he looks less than thrilled to see me. Red faced and sweating, the two damp patches spreading from under his armpits telling a pro like me he's terrified by teenagers and just about managing to keep control, he instantly goes on the attack.

"You're late."

Don't you just love it when teachers state the obvious? I give him my very best bothered? look.

"I'm here now."

There's a little ripple of interest and I spot Emily Lacey regarding me with the cold eyes of a shark looking forward to a kill.

"You're still late," says my tutor. "I take it you're Amber Evans gracing us with your presence?"

"I'm not Batman," I say and there's a titter from the students.

The teacher's face turns an even deeper shade of puce.

"I'm not sure I like your attitude, young lady. However, since it's your first day we'll put it down to nerves. Your uniform, however, I can't quite fathom. Let me explain the concept of uniform, shall I? It's something you wear to school that we've agreed on. A blazer? Dark shoes? A tie?"

I left for Cornwall so abruptly that of course I haven't got a uniform. I've hardly even got any clothes with me. Mum hadn't made it to the launderette for weeks and all I could do was grab the few clean bits I could find and hope that I got home to do the laundry soon. Dogood might have promised social services would give money to my new foster parents for clothes but she wasn't the one having to go to a new school dressed in the odd bits left in the airing cupboard. I can't even remember buying these red leggings I've got on today. I reckon they came back from the hospital by mistake. That happens a lot with Mum; she goes in with her own things and comes out with a load of jumble. I did try sewing her name on to a few bits but it didn't make any difference.

I really hope somebody's looking after her now.

Anyway, Kate's promised to sort me out with a uniform although there's no point since I won't be sticking around. She's written me a note to excuse my leggings and trainers so that I don't, in her words, get told off. That tells you everything you ever needed to know about just how clueless Kate Crewe is. She actually thinks my having a note will stop the teachers having a go which would be sweet really if it wasn't so naïve. She really has no idea that they yell first and read notes afterwards…

I open my mouth to say that I have a note but, surprise surprise, he's got in first because he looks me up and down and than says,

"Or maybe you've come in fancy dress today? Not as Batman though. More like Superman in those tights. Tell me, Amber, which part of today's outfit did you think was appropriate for school? Or anywhere decent?"

The way he says this makes it sounds as though I've rocked up dressed like a Playboy Bunny rather than in leggings, boots and a hoodie. My face starts to grow warm as the other kids snigger.

"I've got a note," I begin but he's lost interest now and returns his attention to the register.

"We'll talk about this over a break time detention."

I've lost my break already?

"But I've got a note!"

"It's not up for discussion. The uniform rule isn't negotiable. Now go and sit down. You can take that nose stud out too."

I pointedly ignore this instruction and glance around the room. Now I'm no mathematical genius but even I can see that thirty students and thirty chairs means there's no room for me.

"Where shall I sit?"

The teacher frowns as he realises too late that there's no extra seat for me.

"Sit on the floor for now and we'll sort something out for later."

The floor? Is he kidding? It's covered in old gum, spit pellets and goodness knows what. No way.

"I'm not sitting on the –" I start to protest but my objection pushes my new tutor over the edge.

"Who do you think you are? How dare you refuse to follow my instructions?" he roars. "It's bad enough waltzing in late looking as though you've come straight from the Oxfam shop! This is not a good start to your time here! Get out and wait in the corridor. The Head of Year can deal with you."

His Oxfam shop comment feels like a punch into my stomach. Charity shops are exactly where Mum buy most of our clothes. I hear Emily laughing and my throat is tight again because how can I explain the truth when he won't listen or even read my note? It doesn't matter what school I'm in; it's always the same story. This is why I always have to get in first with teachers.

I don't wait to be asked twice to get out. Try keeping me in there anyway. Before he can say anything else I'm out of that room and running through the corridors, twisting and turning until at last I spot some fire doors and shove my way outside. Then I'm tearing across the playground and through the gates, my breath coming in painful gasps and a stitch stabbing my side. I don't stop though. I'm getting as far away from this dump as I can.

I'm not sure where I'm going. I don't even know where I am. Kate drove me here and I didn't pay much attention to her route. I slow down, with my heart slamming against my ribs, and bend over to try and gasp some air back into my lungs. I was in such a rush to get out of school I hadn't even noticed that it's raining and not a light drizzle either but a driving downpour which slices through me. I'm absolutely drenched, my hair is plastered against my cheeks and I'm shivering like Mum when she ... when she...

Anyway. I'm cold. I'm wet. And I haven't got a clue where I am. There's probably one bus a week in this place and even if one comes past I don't know where I'm going. St Perran is the nearest village but Kate's farm was miles past there. I suppose I'd better start walking.

I set off, my head bowed against the rain and my hands shoved into my hoody pockets, and soon I'm so cold that I don't even feel them. A sign tells me St Perran is seven miles away so I guess I've got a long walk ahead of me to get back to the farm. If I make it back without catching pneumonia/being run over by a tractor/drowned I'll tell Kate I'm not setting foot in that school again and she can call Dogood and send me home. Stuff Harry and stuff our deal. I'm out of here.

I'm so deep in thought that I've not noticed the muddy Land Rover drawing alongside me in the wet lane.

"Are you OK? You're drenched!"

The window hisses down and I jump when I realise the driver is calling to me.

"Hey! It's you! The girl from the woods! Don't just stand there getting wet! Hop on in!" calls none other than Drake Owen.

CHAPTER 5

"It's OK, I'm not some weirdo who picks up drenched girls," Drake says. "We met yesterday when you were looking at the horses, remember? My name's Drake and you liked my horse, Monty."

"Yeah, I remember. Your girlfriend tried to flatten me."

"Ah, don't take that to heart - it's just Emily's way."

"Seriously? What kind of a psycho is she?"

"One whose father pays my wages," he grins. "And, FYI, I'm her trainer not her boyfriend. If you get in the car before you freeze to death you'll be perfectly safe from her, I promise."

I'm not convinced. Drake may not be Emily's boyfriend but I'm sure she's got him lined up for the job and in my experience girls like her usually get what they want.

"I'm fine," I say. "I like walking."

"In the pouring rain and without a coat?" He shakes his head. "I doubt that. It's dangerous too – visibility's shocking in these lanes and you'll probably be run over. What kind of guy would I be if I let that happen? Please, let's not argue. Just get in."

He reaches across and opens the passenger door. A blast of warm air hits me and I'm lost. Fine I'll take my chances with Emily Lacey if it means I get to ride back to Kate's in dry car. As Drake shoves a pile of *Horse and Hound* magazines out the way and orders two Jack Russells to get onto the back seat, I hop in. He pulls away and I settle onto a patched heavy weight rug, shake the rain back from my hair and fasten my seat belt.

"I'll turn the heating up," Drake is saying, fiddling with the air conditioning vents which cough out hair and dust as well as warmth. The Land Rover smells of horses and feed and damp rugs and I inhale deeply because these scents send me right back to a lost time. "There, that should warm you up a bit. Sorry about about the dog hair, Luke and Leila are terrors for shedding."

I would reply but my teeth are chattering too much and besides being this close to one of my all time idols is robbing me of any coherent though. This is *the* Drake Owen who won Badminton on his eighteenth birthday. He's already legend in the equine world and I can't believe I've met him. The girls I used to have riding lessons with would pop if they knew.

Then a thought occurs: Drake's also the person Harry blames for his father's death. If Harry finds out I'm fraternizing with the enemy I'll be even more unpopular, something I would have said was impossible...

I push this idea aside. I'll be leaving here soon anyway so what does it matter what Harry thinks?

Drake passes me a wad of tissue. "Your makeup's run a bit. You might want to fix it?"

I pull down the passenger sun visor and peer in the vanity mirror. With my white face, mascara smeared cheeks and black hair plastered against my head I look like the undead so I dab at my eyes and do my best to repair it. By the time I've finished I actually feel ten times worse. Ginger eyelashes aren't a good look and without foundation my freckles stand out like bruises.

"So, you know who I am," Drake continues as the car splashes along the lane, "but I don't still know your name. Shall I guess? How about Rumplestiltskin?"

"That's amazing. How on earth did you know?" I deadpan.

He taps his nose. "I'm afraid my sources are classified. Besides, you look like a Rumplestiltskin. It suits you."

"It so does not!"

"It does. You are a bit rumpled. Yep, I'd say it's definitely you. Look, you'd better tell me your real name or I'll be calling you Rumple for the rest of the journey," he warns.

I can't help it; I laugh. Oh dear. It appears that it's hard to be sullen with him around.

"I'm Amber."

"Nice to meet you, Amber," Drake says, changing gear as we drop into a deep valley. "So, where are you going in such a hurry that you couldn't wait for the rain to stop?"

Thank goodness I'm not wearing uniform. That would be a dead giveaway that I'm doing a runner. I don't know Drake Owen and he can't be much more than nineteen but there's something rather old fashioned about him that makes me suspect he'd turn the car around and drive me back to school if he knew I was truanting. Luckily years of dealing with Dogood and co have made me an expert in evading tricky questions.

"Perranview Farm." I look sideways at him just in case there's a reaction at this but not so much as one of his dark eyelashes flicker. Interesting.

"The Crewes' place? That's just along from where I'm headed. I work at Rectory Stables. I'm just on my way back there actually. I'll drop you off." He glances across at me thoughtfully. "Are you staying with them?"

He's pigeon holing me as one of Kate's charity cases and instantly I'm on the defensive.

"What's this? An interrogation?"

"Nope. Just making conversation," he says evenly. "I won't bother if it upsets you though."

Drake switches on the radio and music fills the awkward silence that has fallen. That's my specialty, making people feel uncomfortable, but it's a bit of an own goal this time because I would have liked to have asked him about his horses and how it feels to ride some of the world's most challenging cross country courses. Is there the same swoop of nerves mingled with exhilaration when you turn towards the Cottesmore Leap that I used to feel kicking on towards a jump in the school? Does he also live for those moments sailing through the air?

I suppose I'll never know now.

I fold my arms and stare ahead. The windscreen wipers swipe backwards and forwards and we sit in silence. The rain is easing and as the car climbs again I spot the sea in between a dip in the hills and St Perran clustered around it. Far on the horizon a slice of sunshine peeps out from behind the cloud and spills gold across the water. It's pretty I suppose, in a miles from anywhere kind of way.

Drake is humming along to the radio. He doesn't seem at all bothered by me and I feel a twinge of guilt for being ungrateful. Mum would tell me off for that. He was only trying to help. The trouble is that being defensive has become a bit of a habit. If I get in first I'm left in peace and generally it's a successful strategy. The only problem is that this is a bit rubbish when you realise you'd actually quite like to talk to the person you've been rude to.

I'm just searching for a way to put things right when a big lorry comes around the corner and forces Drake to pull in tightly against the hedge. The cab has HORSES written above it in huge white letters and as it crawls past I crick my neck to try and get a glimpse of what might be inside. It's a childhood habit I can never shake off. And whenever I see a trailer or a lorry I play a guessing game. Is it a dressage horse? A show jumper? Somebody's much loved pony?

Drake frowns. "Damn. They're early."

"That lorry's for you? Is it a new horse? An eventer?"

He raises his eyebrows. "Now who's doing the interrogating?"

I flush and share down at my hands, curled into fists in my lap.

"But since you ask, yes it is a new horse," Drake says, taking pity on me. "It's not for me. This one's a potential eventer for Emily and from the same bloodlines as a couple of Grand Slam winners. If she puts the work in I think he could be something really special. He's tricky, though, which is why I've managed to pick him up fairly cheaply. Horses as talented as Chances don't come up for sale very often otherwise."

I take all this in. I don't know Emily but I have a feeling that she and hard work aren't particularly well acquainted. Still, I should imagine she'll get Drake to do the graft and then pop on and claim the glory. Isn't that what her dad's paying him for?

Drake looks at his watch.

"I'm supposed to be there taking delivery. Are you OK if I drop you off at the Rectory? It's only a short walk to the farm and the sun look's like it's coming out. You can dry out in the tack room and grab a cup of tea first, of course."

"Can I see the horses?" These words are out of my mouth before I can even register them. Oh great, Amber. You sound about twelve. Lennie was cooler when he asked George if he could tend the rabbits.

But Drake doesn't sneer at me in the slightest.

"Absolutely. Be my guest," he agrees, somehow managing to do a three point turn without wedging us in the lane. "Watch out though. If you stick around too long I'll be getting you to muck out."

"It's been a while since I last mucked out."

"You know about horses?"

"A bit."

"Well, then you're my new best friend," Drake says. "Especially if you can clean tack too."

It's been years since I cleaned any tack but I haven't forgotten soaping the leather and sponging clean cheek pieces and nosebands before piecing the bridle back together like a puzzle. I used to spend ages up at the yard helping with the chores and I loved every minute. Dad would leave me there all day and the hours just flew.

It feels like another life.

The lorry trundles ahead. Even from inside the car I can hear the hooves slamming against the partition and the shrill whinnies. I feel a tug of sympathy; this horse is about as happy to be coming here as I was.

"I hope he hasn't been doing that all the way from Sussex," Drake says, grimacing.

The horse kicks again but then the lorry swings left through a pair of huge gates and the shift in balance stops him. We follow it along a sweeping drive, hemmed with post and rail paddocks filled with horses. The Rectory is at the farthest end but the drives forks just before the lawn and leads around to a picture perfect stable yard complete with hanging baskets and a cockerel weather vane. Several inquisitive heads peer out over loose box doors and the new horse shouts again before giving the side of the lorry another hefty kick as it pulls up.

Drake winces. "He'll injure himself at this rate – if he hasn't already."

He parks alongside the lorry and moments later is out of the car and lowering the ramp. I follow him and watch as he ducks inside.

"Rather him than me," says the driver conversationally. "That thing's been going mental since Exeter."

There's more whinnying and kicking from inside the lorry and I can hear Drake doing his best to sooth the horse. There's another hefty kick, a shout as the lead rope is snatched through Drake's hands followed by a loud slamming against the partitions. Then a chestnut Arabian explodes down the ramp, hooves stamping, ear piercing snorts splitting the air and with his mane flying upwards like flames. The weak sun turns his coat to fire and I gasp because I've never seen such a stunning horse in my life. Even trailing a lead rope behind him and with travel boots sliding from his legs, this horse moves with the fluid grace of a ballerina. Just several strides carry him across the yard before he leaps the corner of the Land Rover's bonnet and skids over to one of the stabled horses, spinning on his hocks and sending gravel flying upwards when she lunges at him with bared teeth..

I don't think twice; I'm after him and catching hold of the lead rope before Drake is even on his feet and out of the lorry.

"It's OK, boy," I whisper, placing my hand on his hot neck and scratching it down towards his withers. His veins are tight cords beneath his satin coat and I feel him quivering beneath my finger tips. He's terrified and the more terrified he becomes the more he'll lash out.

Trust me on this one. I know how these things go.

"Sssh," I say. "Steady, now. It's going to all be fine, Chances. You'll see."

The horse snorts again and pulls away sharply, his eyes still rolling. Instinctively, I loosen my hold on the lead rope to take the pressure off and carry on speaking gently until he lowers his head and huffs at me curiously. Still talking, I raise my hand back to the hot neck and scratch some more while liquid eyes regard me warily and oat sweet breath flutes against my cheeks.

"That's the way. Good boy." I run my hand down his neck and feel the tension slide away from him. Like a coiled spring, this horse has been wound up so tightly that all he can do is ping. Anger and shouting and getting upset won't help him now; only calmness can bring anyone this upset back from the brink.

"I wish I had a piece of carrot or a Polo," I tell him. "Maybe that would help you see that hanging out with humans isn't all bad."

"It will be if he knocks me flying like that again," Drake says grimly, rejoining me and rubbing at his arm.

"He was frightened." I'm running my hand down Chances' jaw now, still scratching gently and rubbing the groove under his chin until he starts to lick and chew just like the riding school ponies always did. "Imagine how he must feel, taken away from everything he knows, shoved in a lorry and moved here. That's no fun. It's hardly surprising you're upset, is it boy?"

"Sounds to me like you know what you're talking about." Drake regards me thoughtfully but I don't respond. Firstly, it's none of his business and secondly I'm far too busy talking soothing nonsense to the horse to reply. Drake doesn't say anything else but leans against the stable door, absent mindedly scratching the neck of an interested dapple grey until the new arrival's flanks stop heaving and Chances is finally standing quietly.

"I'm impressed, Amber Rumplestiltskin," he says slowly. "Not many people could have handled that as well as you just did."

I'm surprised because I just did what I always do; imagine how the animal must feel and do my best to make it better.

"I didn't do anything special."

But Drake shakes his head. "I think I'll be the judge of that. He's a tricky one, I'll have a beauty of a bruise to prove that much, and you did exactly the right thing with him."

Praise from Drake Owen about how I've dealt with a horse? I feel my face get hot and I focus on stroking Chances' velvet soft nose.

"So you know about horses then?" he continues. "Tack cleaning skills aside, can you ride?"

"A bit," I admit. "I used to have lessons as a kid but it all stopped when my dad left. There wasn't a lot of money left for things like that after he went and I was busy looking after..." the feed bucket throat lump is back and I gulp it back the way I always do – by not talking about things. "Anyway, I don't ride anymore."

"Well, you should," Drake says firmly. "If you can ride half as well as you can handle horses then you'll be brilliant. Do you fancy a job?"

I look up and he's staring at me, dark eyes narrowed speculatively. Framed by the stable door and with a grey thoroughbred beside him he looks so ridiculously like one of his posters from a pony magazine that I start to laugh.

"I'm serious," he insists. "That wasn't a joke. We could do with a hand. What do you say?"

I'd say that I must be dreaming. I'm also seriously tempted to take him up on it. Imagine working with these beautiful horses every day. I lean my head against Chances' warm neck and for a moment I imagine I'm riding him, pushing him onwards towards a jump and feeling the power and molten fire of speed beneath me as he soars up and over as though flying...

Then I remember dreams are all these ideas will ever because I'm not staying here, am I? The reality is that I'm truanting from my new school on my very first day and when Kate finds out she's going to kick me out and send me back to Bristol where I'll sort Mum out and get things back to normal. Or our version of it anyway. And we all know that normal on the Shakespeare Estate doesn't involve riding three day eventers or spending time with gorgeous guys like Drake. No. The nearest I'll ever get to a horse there is watching the morning line when I walk past Ladbrokes while doing my paper round.

I feel a sharp stab of regret which makes me so angry because it's all right for people like Drake Owen, isn't it? I bet he was born with a whole stable full of gorgeous horses. What does he know about real life? What does he understand about wanting something so badly and knowing that you can never, ever have it?

I shove the lead rope at him and step away.

"No thanks," I snap.

And then I spin around on my heel and turning my back on him and Chances to storm down the drive. I can feel them both watching me all the way to the lane and it takes every inch of self control I posses not to turn around, run back and say *yes please*.

The sooner I get away from here the better.

CHAPTER 6

"Where have you been?"

Kate's waiting for me when I arrive back at the farm house. I had rather hoped she'd be out cleaning or milking cows or whatever it is she does but no such luck. The school's obviously phoned and told her that I walked out. I can tell this because her face is tight with worry. Doesn't look good to lose your new foster child on the second day, I suppose. She probably thought I was hitching a ride back to Bristol.

"The school called," Kate continues. "I've been really worried. They said you left at ten past nine. That was ages ago."

I'm grudgingly impressed my new school's so on the ball. Nobody notices if I don't turn up at my usual place. Or maybe they do but are so glad I'm not in that they don't make a fuss?

Now there's a thought.

"I was walking back," I say. "It's a long way."

The truth is that after leaving Drake I couldn't face anyone. I felt all shaken up, like a can of Coke in a rucksack, and I knew that if anyone said the wrong thing I would fizz everywhere. Instead of coming straight back to the farm I followed the lane out to the orchard where I'd found a relatively dry patch under the trees. Treacle meandered over and nudged me for titbits and I scratched his neck for a bit until he grew bored and returned to his grazing. Then I sat with my back against the damp bark and watched him until my heart beat slowed and I felt less likely to explode.

Gnawing worry had soon replaced my bad temper. What on earth was I doing here, sitting under a tree moping? I didn't have time for this. I messaged my neighbour to check on Scally, who was fine, and then I sent Mum a text but there was no reply. Maybe she didn't feel like talking or maybe she was asleep? At least I knew she was safe, which was something, I supposed. I didn't have much credit left so I didn't try again. Besides, I didn't know when I might need to make a call so I needed to save what little I still did have.

Now I'm back Kate looks as though she wants to say more but just manages to stop herself in time.

"You look frozen," is all she says, ushering me into the kitchen and sitting me on the tatty sofa beside the Aga while she makes tea. Harry, already at the table and chowing down on a massive sandwich, gives me a look which could curdle the milk his mum's pouring into my mug.

"Day one and already truanting," he remarks. "Could she be any more predictable, we ask?"

I ignore him. I hadn't realised how cold I was until I came inside. My fingers actually ache as the heat hits them. Saffy comes and leans against me and her heavy body feels solid and warm.

Kate shoots him a warning look. "Not now, love."

"Yes, now," Harry says. He pins me with a clear blue eyed gaze. "Mum's been worried sick. She even got me to go out looking for you incase you were dead in a hedge somewhere."

He doesn't add *no such luck* but I can tell he's thinking it.

"I didn't ask you to do that," I mutter.

"No, Mum did!" Harry snaps. "Jeez, as if she's not got enough to worry about without you being such a cliché. We all know you were brought here kicking and screaming. You don't have to labour the point."

An image of Chances, hooves slicing through the air and whinnying shrilly, flashes through my mind's eye. I wonder if he's settled?

"This has been a big upheaval for Amber," Kate says gently, passing me a mug of tea.

"She's nearly sixteen. She knows the score," Harry replied. "It's not like we're the first foster family she's been placed with, is it?"

Hardly. Fifth? Sixth? With any luck the Crewes will be the last. Once I'm sixteen it's a whole different ball game.

Kate leans against the Aga rail and smiles wearily. "But hopefully you're going to like it here, Amber. I know it's miles away from home and a big change but we'll do our best to make it all OK."

Harry snorts. "You might. I'm not running around her. She's big enough to know that this is a cushy number and if she isn't?" He shrugs his broad shoulders and looks me full in the eye. "Well, let's just say it's time you stopped trying to save the world, Mum, and gave bed and breakfast a try. I bet those guests would at least be gracious and I wouldn't have to stop ploughing to sort them out. Why bother with somebody who's just having a strop?"

"I wasn't having a strop!" I glare at him and at this exact moment I actually think I hate Harry for so easily dismissing the hassle I've had this morning. It's all right for him with his tractor and his mum and his own life.

Nobody's had a go at him about looking like he dresses in a charity shop, have they? For a second I'm tempted to tell them what really happened at school then I remind myself that there's no point. I'm not staying anyway so why do they need to know?

"That's enough, Harry." Kate's voice is quiet but firm. To me she says, "I was worried about you, Amber. You don't know the area and you could have been anywhere. You could have been knocked down."

"I wasn't anywhere. I was at the Rectory Stables with Drake," I say. "He gave me a lift back and showed me the horses."

"Drake Owen. I might have known he'd be involved." Harry shoves his plate away as though just the mention of Drake is enough to ruin his appetite. "How typical. Now he's encouraging school kids to truant."

"I'm not a school kid!"

Harry's blonde eyebrows rise. "You certainly behave like one and we can't deny you're a truant."

He should be a lawyer, not a farmer.

"Drake didn't encourage me to truant. He gave me a lift back," I say. "He's not done anything wrong."

"Ha!" Harry explodes from the table and starts to pace. The drama of this is ruined a bit because he's wearing woolly socks but standing up he's a lot taller than I realised and his anger seems to fill the kitchen. "Not done anything wrong? That's a good one. Where shall we start?"

"This is nothing to do with Amber," Kate points out quickly.

"It is if she's decided he's her new best friend," Harry hisses. "It's time she knew the truth."

I stare at him. Harry was techy with me yesterday but this is something else. White hot rage seems to consume him and his eyes are gas flame blue.

"What truth?" I ask. Is this what Maddy was telling me about? That Drake Owen killed their father? I'd thought that was just a little kid exaggerating. I can't see Drake Owen as a killer.

Not unless his good looks make girls drop dead with longing anyway…

"Harry," says Kate but her son ignores the warning tone.

"She needs to know, Mum, especially if we're going to be stuck with her." He stops his pacing and his hands bunch into fists. Harry's cheekbones are stained pink, and his breathing's ragged. "Drake's father killed mine. That's the truth."

Is he serious?

"It's not quite that simple," Kate begins but Harry turns on her furiously.

"Yes it is! When will you stop making excuses?" To me he says, "My dad was always working to try and make ends meet. Foot and mouth nearly wiped us out in my granddad's day and ever since then we've been struggling. To earn extra money, Dad used to work for other farmers fencing or ploughing – extra hands are always needed. He was working on the Owens' farm when there was a fatal tractor accident."

My dad was squashed by a tractor.

"What happened?" I ask.

"Ben was killed." Kate slumps at the table and places her face in her hands. She seems to sag, little more than sad heap of flowery smock, cheap jeans and a mop of hair greying at the roots. "It was an accident. A terrible, terrible accident."

"Except that an enquiry showed their machinery hadn't been properly maintained," Harry says angrily. "The Owens had been cutting corners. The court case might have recorded an open verdict but we all know it was their fault. Dad died because of them. Their negligence and greed cost my father his life."

Harry's voice breaks and he looks away. I know he's fighting not to lose control and I totally get that. The feeling of your throat tightening and your eyes prickling is a familiar one. I usually resort to my earring trick but Harry has to rely on sheer will power. I'm grudgingly impressed: he must be a really strong guy.

"The Owens had to sell their farm to cover their legal costs but there was no compensation for us. Dad had let his life insurance lapse too so the rest you can probably figure out. Drake was desperate to find a place to keep his horses so he went to Michael and I quit college to run our farm."

Kate takes his hand.

"I know how much you gave up, love."

"I'd do it again in a heartbeat," says Harry fiercely. "But I never forget who's to blame. Never. And I'll never let anyone else hurt my family."

The message is clear but somehow I find I don't resent hearing it. Kids protecting their mums is something I totally get. I can't help thinking it's a bit unfair Drake's blamed for what his father did (I'd be in trouble if the same was true for me) but I like Harry's loyalty.

I feel bad for upsetting Kate. She's got a whole set of her own problems without having to deal with mine too. I'm not such a lost cause that I can't feel sympathy for other people.

"I'm sorry, Kate," I say. "I didn't know."

She sighs. "You didn't need to know, love. These aren't your problems."

But Harry flings me a sharp look that says they will be if I mess up again. I know I'm not staying here and that I want to get kicked out but I don't want to cause Kate Crewe any more grief. It sounds as though she's had quite enough already and goodness knows why she wants to volunteer for more by taking in people like me. It's all very noble but Harry's right: bed and breakfast makes far more sense.

"I won't truant again," I promise, silently adding *while I'm at that school.* "I'll stick it out while I'm here. That won't be long anyway. My mum will be better soon."

"Since I've confessed all our deepest secrets, what's the deal with your mum? How come you're in foster care?" Harry asks.

Kate is horrified. "Harry Crewe! You can't ask Amber that!"

"I just did," he says. "So?"

"It's on a needs to know base only," I say automatically. This is my usual defense but Harry isn't buying it. Instead he sits down at the table and regards me thoughtfully through narrowed eyes.

"Fine. Since this is our *Jeremy Kyle* moment we might as well be honest. And anyway, I think I do *need to know*. If you're going to be such a pain in the butt while we're stuck with you then I may as well try and understand why."

"Now I know why you're a pain in the butt, you mean?" I counter.

Harry grins and it's like the sun is coming out from behind clouds. Oh, what the heck? I may as well tell him. I'll be gone soon so what does it matter if he knows the truth? He thinks I'm a lost cause anyway.

"My mum's in hospital right now. She's mental. A nutter. A loony. Psycho. There. Happy? Good enough reasons for you?"

I know my words are ugly but I want to shock him. These names are what people on our estate call Mum. They don't understand the truth like I do. They don't know how fragile and sweet she really is, how if I'm not there to make sure she takes her tablets then she starts to fray at the edges. They haven't watched her rock and cry and talk to people who aren't here. They haven't come home from school to find her unconscious with an empty bottle clutched in her hand. They haven't seen…seen…

Anyway. That.

Is is any wonder I can't leave her? Once Dad walked out how could I go anywhere for long? She needs me.

Harry stares at me. Take that, farm boy. If we're playing *Rubbish Family Trumps* then I raise my mad mum against your dead dad. Next?

"Anything else you need to know?" I demand.

He shakes his head. "Err, no. Thanks."

"Amber's mum, Sara, had a severe breakdown a few years ago," Kate explains gently, which is a nicer way of saying it and the expression Dogood favours. "She's very unwell again now and she needs to be in hospital where they can take specialist care of her."

That's another way of putting it, I guess. It's not what the graffiti on our stair well said, though. And for *in hospital* read *sectioned*.

Put it this way; Mum didn't exactly go quietly…

"It's technically called psychotic depression," I say bluntly. Take that.

"Sara's been very unwell and she might be in hospital for a month or two this time, which is why Amber's come here." Kate gives me an encouraging smile. "It's not forever though, love. Your mum will be out of hospital soon, I'm sure."

She will. I can guarantee it. Mum is constantly in and out of hospital. She's like the NHS's version of the Okey Cokey. I'm used to it though because I've been looking after her for a long time. That said, she has been especially bad lately and Dogood did say she could be in the hospital for a while. Hence me needing long term care and having to come here.

The irony of that, eh? *I'm* usually the one who gives the care to *her.* Nobody usually looks after me so I'm not sure what the difference is just because Mum's in hospital. If anything, my life's slightly less complicated with the doctors taking care of her.

Harry doesn't say much more after this. He pulls his overalls and boots back on and returns to the farm work while Kate meets Maddy from the bus. I wander outside and poke around the yard for a bit but it's pretty depressing because everything's looking tired. From the flaking paint to the gates tied with string to the weed choked flower beds, Perranview Farm is in a bad way. I hide away in my attic bedroom for the rest of the afternoon, ignoring Maddy when she calls to me, and staring up at the ceiling. Talking about Mum has brought everything into really sharp focus and the events of the past couple of days play out again. I feel for Harry and Kate and Maddy, I do. I really do. But Mum has to be my priority.

I don't know how long I lie on my bed. Long enough for the sun to start to sink. It's only when I hear the metallic clatter of horse shoes on tarmac and a shout that I move. Crossing the room to the window, my heart skips a beat when I see a horse cantering sideways down the road, foam like egg white flying from his mouth and with his head yanked in with a bungee cord. The rider holds the reins so tightly that all the horse can do is dance and spin and each time he does she brings her whip down with a thwack on his shoulder before jabbing her spurs into his heaving flanks.

It's Chances and Emily.

Emily's face is tense and her hands are set on the reins. There's no sign of Drake and I wonder if he even knows she taken the new arrival out. Somehow I doubt it. The horse should have been left to settle in after his long journey, not booted round the lanes. He needed space and quiet. Time to work out his new surroundings and just to be a horse. That's basic common sense, surely? With every yank from the rider he's becoming more tense and he's the kind who only becomes sharper the more upset he gets. That floating trot and tossing head might look impressive but the horse surging and plunging beneath the rider is deeply unhappy.

"Stop jogging!" I hear Emily snap as she slaps the crop down onto his neck. Sweat foams, the veins stand out and I can hardly bear to watch. Every jab of the reins in that peach soft mouth makes me flinch and I feel my own pulse accelerate with each pinched step.

Maddy has slipped into my room and is watching Emily riding away.

Her pale face is sad.

"Emily's really mean," she says.

I look at the horse, strapped down and bitted up, and being walloped for nothing more than protesting at the bad riding and discomfort. Yes, I think it's true to say that Emily Lacey is very mean. I wish I could do something to help the horse and Maddy too. But what can I do?

How can somebody like me possibly compete with the girl who has everything?

CHAPTER 7

If I'd thought things were bad on my first day at school, it's nothing compared to the rest of my week. Kate manages to cobble a uniform together so at least my form tutor leaves me alone. In the meantime, Emily does a great job of shooting me evil looks and making nasty comments when the teachers aren't paying attention and has even *accidentally* spilled her drink in my bag. The rest of the kids are either too scared or too stupid to stand up to her so my first week at my new school is about as miserable as a first week can be.

I've texted Mum a few times but there's still no reply. This means she's either too ill to text, which really worries me, or she's not paid her bill and has been cut off. That's way more likely but I need to know for sure so, in a fit of desperation, I even call Dogood. This turns out to be pointless because she only tells me I mustn't worry and everything's going fine with Mum and she's in the best place yada yada yada. I'm unconvinced because as far as I can see things are about as far from fine as they can possibly get. I do manage to reach my neighbour, Lynn, who tells me Scally's fine but as the days roll by and there's no sign of anyone coming to fetch me home I realise that this is serious. Mum is in hospital for a while this time, there really isn't any where for me to go in Bristol and like it or not, I'm going to be stranded in Cornwall for the foreseeable.

After my conversation with Harry and Kate I feel a little wrong footed. I can see how hard Kate works to try and keep everything together at the farm and I can't help admiring how Harry has taken over from his father in order to make her life easier. Harry works long hours, he's always up and gone long before Maddy and I catch the school bus, and he's never back indoors before dark. If Harry wishes he could be at college or living a normal eighteen-year-old life, he never says so. He never complains.

But you don't do you? Not when you're trying your best to look after someone you love.

I also see how much work the house and farm must take and I soon realise that flaking paint and broken hinges are the least of Kate's problems. The house is warm, there's always lots of food and the animals are well loved. The mud, dirty windows and air of shabby resignation all make perfect sense now. Everyone's doing their best to make things work and pay to bills. Even Maddy collects eggs and cleans the hens out before school as well as having a list of chores to complete when she gets home. Kate's out cleaning a lot of the time and when she isn't she's working on the farm too or tending the vegetable patch. My tried and tested master plan of being so difficult that my foster family can't wait to send me home suddenly feels a little unfair.

In fact, worse than that. It feels totally wrong.

This is very bad news indeed for me because it means I am well and truly stuck until either a placement is found for me in Bristol, Mum gets better or I turn sixteen. I could be here a while.

At least Harry and Maddy can help Kate. I'm just seen as another problem my mum has to worry about. The social workers actually think *she* worries about *me* and view me as a hindrance. That hurts when I know it's me who's kept everything together. Goodness only knows what I'll come home to. No after school jobs. No way of paying the bills. No keeping the house clean for weeks on end. We've probably got squatters by now.

Dogood can say what she likes; it's all going to be ten times worse.

So on top of of worrying about Mum and Scally and the mess that I'll come home to, the last thing I need is Emily Lacey being a cow. For some reason she's totally taken against me, probably because I dared look at her horses. and she's going out of her way to make my life a misery. The whispers of 'skank', rumour that I'm a gypsy and all the nasty comments about being another reject from Kate's farm, I can ignore. I've met bigger and nastier than her before – you don't survive the Shakespeare Estate without learning to pick your battles – and the deliberate knocking of my books onto the floor and the sniggers I can handle. I can even just about control my temper but the one thing I know I can't handle is her knowing the truth. That would be unbearable. People can laugh at me all they like. I can take it. But laugh at Mum? No way. I hope she never finds out.

I keep all this to myself. Nobody would believe me anyway. Emily's one of those butter wouldn't melt types that teachers love and I know they'll never listen to me. Why would they? I've been pegged as a trouble maker from day one. My form tutor must have had a bollocking for his 'charity shop' comment because he barely acknowledges me. I even wear my nose piercing but he just ignores it. My last school hasn't sent my academic records across and so I've been placed in all the bottom sets where I spend most of my time doing word searches and colouring in while a supply teacher cowers in the corner. I stick it this out as best I can but it's pretty soul destroying. Sometimes I get myself sent to exclusion just for some peace and quiet. At least there I can read without having to dodge flying text books and paper aeroplanes.

And as for becoming a vet? I think we can safely say that won't happen now. My GCSE results aren't going to set any records, that's for sure.

By the middle of the second week I can't take much more. Luckily I've figured out the buses so I hop off with Maddy then, once she's safely inside, nip across the road and retrace my journey. For obvious reasons I can't go back to the farm so instead I walk down the lane, skulking along the hedges so that Harry doesn't spot me from his tractor, before I climb the gate into one of Michael Lacey's paddocks.

The first two days I do this Drake's ex eventer, Monty, and a couple of other horses that must belong Emily are turned out. They trot over with great interest when I first arrive, nudging my coat pockets for treats and huffing warm breath down my neck. Once they realise that I don't have anything more interesting than my bus pass they soon amble away and I find myself a space under the trees at the far end of the paddock. I text my mum, check on Scally and then I do something my English teacher would never believe – I settle down to read my set text. It's amazing just how interesting *Silas Marner* is when you've nothing else to do. The bit about the adopted daughter choosing to stay with him over her real family makes me feel a bit queasy though. I'm never going to let that happen. No matter what, Mum is my mum and I have to be there for her.

Anyway, this morning things go pretty much as usual. Kate drops Maddy and I at the bus stop. We hop off again thirty minutes later. So far so ordinary. Maddy goes in through the gates, I pretend to then cross the road and catch the next bus back. The sun is out today and it's a sparkly autumnal morning. The trees are on the change, orange splodges and gold specks blur by as the bus trundles along, and when I jump off and walk down the lane I can see my breath in the air. Luckily Kate has found me a coat from somewhere other wise I'd be in for a chilly day.

I climb the gate and drop into the paddock, heading for my favourite spot when I realise that somebody is already there. The usual horses have been moved and instead Chances is snoozing beneath the trees. His breath rises in plumes and when he hears me approach he snorts.

I stop in my tracks and the horse and I stare at one another, both wary and both a little put out at having our solitude interrupted. The he trots towards me, a floating magical trot that doesn't even seem to touch the grass, and whickers softly. I don't move but let him sniff me and blow warm breath against my face. Eyes dark and soft as black velvet regard me warily and I know one false move will send him plunging away down the field, hooves flying and tail streaming in the cold wind.

"Hello Chances," I say.

He wickers softly and slowly, holding my breath, I stretch out my hand and touch his neck. The horse quivers under my finger tips. His nostrils flare and every nerve is poised to flee.

"It's OK," I tell him. "I'm not going to hurt you. In fact, I may even have something you'd like."

Without making any sudden movements I slide my fingers into the rucksack I've been given for school and rummage around for the lunch box Kate insists on giving me every day. Yes, seriously. My foster mother actually makes packed lunches. No packets of crisps or chips in the school canteen for her children, home grown or fostered. The first time I peeled back the lid I nearly died of shock to find a sandwich made with home baked bread, a wad of flapjack and an apple. *Jamie Oliver, eat your heart out* I'd thought as I tucked in.

Right now I could give Kate a hug because today's offering contains an apple. Sliding it out, I bite it into chunks which the Arab takes gently from my outstretched palm. While he munches happily I bury my face in his silken mane and breath in the smell of horse. Memories of fat riding school ponies come flooding back and in a heartbeat I'm twelve again, loving my riding and flying over the jumps while my proud parents watch.

It was another life. One before Dad left home and Mum and I had to move into the city and the flat on the estate. There weren't any riding lessons after that.

"Are you in the naughty paddock?" I ask and Chances blows oaty breath at me. I'll take that as a 'yes'. I've seen Emily ride him a couple of times and it doesn't look as though things are going well. The more she tightens the reins or choses a stronger bit the more upset Chances becomes. The horse needs gentleness and understanding, the more tense his rider is the worse he'll become. I can see that so why can't she?

As Chances crops the grass I'm struck by just how unfair life is. Here's Emily with this beautiful horse, fleet of foot and with every line of his body, every twitch of his ears, every movement of his finely boned legs crying out how special he is and all she can do is kick and yank and bully. A horse like Chances can't be bullied. Won't be bullied. Instead he'll fight and fight until something terrible happens. Then he'll be labelled a bad horse, un-rideable, not worth bothering with…

Something starts to blow up inside me. I no longer see the paddock or feel the cold wind against my cheeks. Instead I hear the steady beat of hooves as I gather up my reins and turn towards a jump before soaring over it in a perfect arc…

My rucksack's on the floor and my right hand clutches a chunk of mane. It's been years but that doesn't seem to matter because I remember exactly how to do this. There's a warm and strong back beneath me, the gentle swell of flanks against my legs and the curve of arched neck in front of me. I vault onto his back and Chances doesn't move but just pricks his ears as I lean forward and smooth his neck.

"Hello there boy," I whisper.

I'm on a horse. How many years has it been? Four? Five? A long time anyway but in a weird way it feels like yesterday too. This is the most natural thing in the world and without doubt the best place to be. The coiled power beneath me makes my heart sing and without thinking twice or caring that I don't have any tack, I touch Chances' sides with my heels.

There's a rush of cold air against my face as he explodes into a star fish buck. Hooves flash by my face as I slam onto the ground with a thump that knocks all the breath out of my body. While Chances tears down the paddock I lie in the grass and gasp for air. I don't think I've broken anything but I don't dare move for a moment. Instead, I stay still and try to suck some breath back into my lungs but even as my head pounds and the sky spins above me I'm thinking that with a buck like that Chances could jump Mars. I've never felt such power or such speed in my life. Imagine that pitted against the clock? It would be unbeatable!

I can't wait to try again and this time I'll be ready for him!

"What the Hell are you doing?"

For a moment I think I must have really hit my head hard because this looks and sounds just like Harry. He's bending over me and scowling, which is very Harry because he seems to scowl a lot when I'm around. I sit up and rub my eyes but unfortunately he's still there, wearing his green work overalls and looking furious.

I think, given the choice, I'd have preferred concussion.

"Riding?" I say, although it comes out like a squeak.

"Are you completely mad?"

I shrug. "Maybe. Perhaps it's hereditary?"

"Don't be flippant!" Harry roars. "You could have killed yourself."

Hauling me to my feet, he adds, "Apart from that, which might make my life a lot easier, you're trespassing on Michael's land as well as riding his horse without permission. Do you want to make things even harder for Mum? Do you want to give him even more of an excuse to kick us out?"

I hadn't even thought about this. Vaulting onto Chances had felt as instinctive as breathing. Nothing else mattered.

Harry looks like he wants to shake me until my fillings rattle. He towers over me and I realise just how tall and strong he is. Where Drake Owen is all sinew and honed riding physique, Harry is pure strength and bulked up muscle and power. When he checks me over for injuries like I'm one of the farm animals, I don't protest. Those strong hands could probably snap me in two.

"Anyway, why aren't you in school?" he demands, releasing me while I brush grass and mud off my trousers.

"Why are you spying on me?" I counter.

His top lip curls. "I'd hardly call driving my tractor down the lane *spying*, Amber. More like doing an honest day's work which is something you clearly don't know much about."

I ignore this dig. "So you spooked Chances? Typical."

"So this is my fault? Interesting. Please explain how you work that out since you're a) truanting and b) joy riding?"

I'm aching like crazy from my fall. There wasn't a lot of joy in this ride but next time it's going to be better and there will be a next time, I know that much already.

"Look," I say wearily, "there's no point in me going to school. Trust me on this."

"Says who?" Harry asks. "I thought you were supposed to be some kind of super brain? I've sneaked a peak at your records, just to make sure Mum hasn't taken in a complete psycho, you'd do the same, and they say you're clever. More than clever. Gifted and talented. You told me yourself you want to be a vet. So why truant?"

I look away. Chances is grazing at the far end of the paddock now. The flight of moments earlier is forgotten as he champs at the grass and whisks flies away with his tail. I wish I could leave my upsets behind so easily.

"You wouldn't understand."

"Try me," Harry suggests. "You might be surprised."

I don't know why I tell him. Harry's hardly my friend and he clearly thinks I'm a waste of skin. Maybe it's the fact that he's asked me? Or maybe I walloped my head harder than I realised? In any case as we climb the gate and walk towards his tractor I find myself telling him about Emily and the bottom sets and the wrong uniform. I even tell him how worried I am that Mum isn't answering her texts and that my neighbour says Scally isn't settling. She also says she might have to rehome her because looking after a dog is taking far too much time. I nearly lose it when I get to this bit and I wait for Harry to tell me to pull myself together but he doesn't. Instead, he listens patiently while I blurt it all out in a great big misery vomit.

It's worse when he's nice because now I feel dangerously close to tears and I never cry in front of anyone. Ever.

"Sorry, I didn't mean to dump all that on you," I say. I can't look him in the face because if I see any sympathy I think I'll crack.

"Blimey. Was that an apology? Did you actually say the 's' word?"

Teasing. That's more like it. Teasing I can handle.

I raise my chin.

"As if. I think your ears are playing up."

"Probably," Harry agrees. His lips twitch. "Of course, silly me. I would never have heard that from you."

He pauses and a frown creases his forehead.

"What?"

"I'm just wondering what I can do to help. Can we talk to someone at school about it? Get the teachers to have a word with Emily?"

I laugh bitterly. "Like they'll believe me against her. Come on, Harry. You didn't leave school that long ago. You must remember how it works? Tatty, foster kid with a bad attitude versus the pretty posh girl with the rich daddy? Who do you think they'll believe is the problem? Any interference will just make things a million times worse."

For Maddy as well as me, I add silently.

Harry sighs. "Fine. I've known Emily Lacey long enough to know what you're up against there. But Emily aside, what about your lessons? They can't just dump you in the bottom sets. That isn't fair."

"Since when did fair come into it? They can and they have." I force myself to look unconcerned. "Hey, it happens every time I change school so don't worry about it. It's not your problem."

"That's where you're wrong," Harry says grimly. "The thing is, Amber, if you truant then it's Mum who's called to account and I can't have any more stress on her. It isn't fair."

Harry's right; it isn't. I know that.

"We both know how these things work," he continues, folding his arms and looking at me thoughtfully. "You're nearly sixteen so they could find you a place in a hostel, couldn't they? If they had to? You could go somewhere else."

Harry certainly knows his stuff. Yesterday Dogood phoned and told me exactly the same thing. Mum isn't being discharged any time soon and there's nowhere else for me to go in Bristol. Our flat isn't an option either. Dogood thought there might be a hostel place at some point but the subtext was clear – I can't go home and I can't rescue Scally.

So if I can't go home then, hard as it is to admit it, I'd rather stay here. At least at Perranview Farm there are animals, horses next door and although Kate might fuss she's a million times better than Auntie Sue. Even Harry isn't too bad, I suppose.

"So shall I drive you back to school and we'll pretend this never happened? Or shall we call your social worker and get you moved to a hostel?" he asks.

I glance across at Chances. The low sunshine turns his coat to fire and when he looks up at me at whinnies I know what my answer is. I have to ride this horse again. I have to.

It looks like I'm going to have to strike another deal with Harry. This is getting to be a habit.

"Take me back to school," I say.

CHAPTER 8

After this encounter with Harry I don't have much choice but to knuckle down. Luckily I'm used to surviving new schools and it's easy enough to keep my head below the parapet. If I pretend I can't hear Emily's snide comments and do my best to stay out of her way, I'll survive my time here. It might look as though I've given in by toning down the makeup and letting my hair colour fade but this is educational chess and my tactics are all about playing the long game. The hardest part is keeping my temper. When I feel it start to bubble I just imagine how it must feel to be Chances, strapped down and jabbed in the mouth, and I know that if he can bear it then so can I. There's got to be a way out for both of us. I just need to figure out what it is.

The only thing that makes life bearable is the Arab. I've been here almost three weeks and as kind as Kate and my social workers are they don't understand how frustrating it feels to be so powerless. Thank God for horses. They don't care who you are or what you've done. Horses only care about being looked after and the treats you bring them. Besides, things aren't so different for Chances, are they? I watch Emily ride past most days and Chances' wild eyes and stamping hooves break my heart because this is a horse of fire, born to gallop like flames licking through dry timber, not to be held in and bullied with harsh bits and gadgets. Short martingales and tight flash nosebands only make him panic. Why can't Emily see that? And why isn't Drake stopping her?

I manage to slip down to Chances' paddock most days and the horse comes cantering over now when I call him. I've always got an apple or a polo in my pocket and while he munches away I whisper nonsense to and scratch his withers. I haven't attempted to sit on him again because my time with Chances is limited to snatched minutes here and there in between school and helping with the animals on the farm, but as soon as I get an opportunity I know I will.

It's Saturday morning and, after a fun filled hour cleaning out chickens and hanging washing, I'm walking down the lane to the paddock with pockets stuffed full of apples. Kate's cleaning, Harry's contracted out working on Michael's estate and Maddy's with him in the tractor, which leaves me free. There's no news of Mum, apart from Dogood's assurances that she's doing well which may or may not be true, and our neighbour's stopped replying to my texts about Scally. I haven't spoken a word about this to anyone, much as Dogood would love me to crack and see the school counsellor. I don't need to do that because I share all my darkest worries with Chances. He's a good listener and he keeps all my secrets too. I'm not saying Harry hasn't keep them but since our last conversation I've stayed away from him. He knows way too much about me now and, in my experience, that's never a good thing. People who get too close only end up letting you down, don't they? Look at my dad, for instance. He's a prime example. Harry's always working anyway and I don't suppose he's even noticed I'm not about. It's not as if he even likes me.

And anyway, why do I care if Harry Crewe doesn't like me? I'm not here to be liked. I'm here because it's only place they could dump me.

I'm just turning left into the lane which hems Michael Lacey's land when I hear the clatter of hoof beats heading towards me at speed. Seconds later Chances flies around the corner with stirrups and reins flying. Sparks fly from his metal shoes, foam flies from his mouth and his nostrils are blood red. There's no sign of any rider but his heaving flanks and sweat flecked neck suggest he's been ridden hard before finally having enough. Having experienced one of his bucks I'm not all surprised his rider has parted company with the saddle.

"Hey, boy! Shhh!"

I don't think twice before stepping out to catch him. Taken by surprise, Chances skitters to a halt before rearing up and striking out with his forelegs. Cold air and a blur of hooves rush past my face as my fingers close around the reins and he snorts loudly.

"It's all right, Chances," I soothe, running my hand down his hot neck. The veins stand up like cords and he trembles beneath my touch. "It's all going to be fine."

Slowly, I feel him relax. I keep soothing and stroking and talking nonsense until Chances lowers his head, rests it on my shoulder and huffs hot breath against my neck. Several chunks of apple seem to cheer him up greatly and before long he's nudging my arm for more.

"What happened?" I murmur as I check his legs. "Did Emily fall off?"

Chances doesn't answer of course but the swinging stirrups and too tight girth speak volumes. I've only met Drake a couple of times but I'm sure he'd never fasten a flash noseband so tightly. I'm no fan of Emily's but

I can't ignore the fact that she might be lying injured and afraid somewhere.

"We have to find her, Chances," I say, gathering the reins into my left hand and placing my foot in the stirrup. "Where did you come from?"

I hop once, twice and swing up into the saddle. My right foot slides easily into the stirrup and although they're a little short for me it feels as though I've been sitting up here all my life. Chances stiffens as he feels my weight on his back and I run my hand down his neck to reassure him.

"It's only me," I say and one chestnut ear flicks backwards at the sound of my voice. "It's all fine, boy. I'm here now."

I hold the reins loosely and I don't even need to use my legs, just shifting my seat a little is enough to send him forwards. The energy and power beneath me is incredible, as far from the tired riding school ponies as it is possible to imagine, and it feels like I'm sitting on a coiled spring. Instantly I understand that tensing up on Chances is doomed to end in disaster so I force myself to relax, breathing slowly and talking to him as we walk down the road. Soon my reins are at the buckle and his head is lower, his jaw relaxed and his hind quarters stepping beneath him rather than crabbing sideways. The snatching of the bit and the dancing in the spot that I've seen so many times are replaced by a smooth stride and happily pricked ears.

Now where did the horse come from? This lane ends at the paddock. To the left are the woods where I first saw Drake and Emily, to the right the drive up to the Rectory. Chances can't have come that way because there's a cattle grid which means Chances must have made his way through the woods. There's no way out except for the five bar gate which he must have jumped before landing in the road and galloping towards the Crewe's farm. Emily could be lying in the woods and nobody has any idea she's there except for me. I suppose I don't have much choice but to retrace Chances' journey.

Which means I'll have to jump the gate.

My stomach flutters. That five bar gate is huge. It must be at least four feet high and it's solid too. The riding school ponies would need a spring board to get over that and I've never jumped anything so big in my life.

Until now.

Before I can think too long about this, I'm gathering up the reins, collecting Chances up and pushing him into a steady canter. I fix my gaze somewhere in the dim greenness of the path beyond and ride at the gate with my heart thudding. Chances surges forward, his ears prick with excitement, there's a rush of air against my face and we're soaring up and over the gate. I don't even have time to register that I've just cleared the biggest jump of my life because we've landed and are speeding along the woodland path in a floating canter that rapidly stretches into a gallop as Chances snatches the reins and heads for home.

The unexpected freedom makes me laugh out loud. Chances is fleet of foot and covers the ground smoothly, twisting and turning along the track and leaping fallen logs and piles of brash. It feels like flying and for a brief moment I forget everything except the horse beneath me and the pure joy of speed. Then I remember why we're actually here and, sinking deeper into the saddle, I ask Chances to steady. He flings his head up into the air, narrowly missing my face, and leaps sideways but when he finds there's no pressure on his mouth and nobody trying to fight him he relaxes into a trot and finally a walk.

I pat his neck with a hand that's shaking with a mixture of adrenalin and excitement.

"Nice to know you have brakes," I say.

Reins loose again, I let Chances pick his way along the track. There's no sign of Emily though. Before long the trees thin out and the Rectory appears. We've covered a mile at least in a loop around Michael Lacey's land and I can't think of anywhere else Chances could have been. He clearly knows his way through the woods and the soft track is scored with hoof prints. If Emily's fallen off here I imagine she's managed to make her way home. Maybe a wallop on the head will have turned her into a nicer person?

We can live in hope, I suppose.

The stables are straight ahead and as we approach Chances whinnies. Several horses answer and he tosses his head and starts to jog and dance. I ride into the yard with a clatter and instantly Drake comes running with Emily, alive and kicking but with tell tale smears of mud on her cream jodhpurs, hard on his heels.

"What on earth are you playing at?" Drake grabs my reins and glowers up at me. "You could have broken your neck!"

I lean forward and pat Chances' glossy neck. The Arab's standing still and it's hard to imagine I'm in any danger.

"Oh chill out," I say airily. "He's been good as gold. We had a great ride back through the woods."

Drake stares at me. "You're telling me you rode him through the woods?"

I nod.

"Where did you find him?"

"Tearing down the lane towards Kate's place. Much further along and he'd have been on the main road."

Drake's eyebrows shoot into his dark hair. "I never thought for a minute he'd jump out on his own. No wonder I couldn't find him in the woods." Then he frowns. "Hold on. How did on earth did you get back in? That gate's always locked. Michael has the only key."

"I thought somebody must have fallen off him in the woods so I popped him over the gate and rode through in case they were hurt," I explain. "Hi, Emily. Glad to see you're not hurt after your tumble. Don't feel bad. It happens to us all."

"Get off my horse!" Emily hisses. If looks could kill I'd be dead at her Dubarry booted feet. "You've got no right to be on him."

"At least I *am* on him though," I say sweetly as I kick my feet out of the stirrups and slide off. Unused to riding after all this time my legs feel like boiled noodles and I stagger as my trainers hit the cobbles. "Tell me, Emily, where did you come off? In the woods? Or at the gate?"

As we bristle at one another, Drake runs a hand through his dark hair and sighs. "Come on girls, cut the squabbling out. Amber, you took a crazy risk riding Chances but we owe you big time for bringing him home and for looking for Emily too, right Em?"

Emily shoots me an ugly look. We both know they'll be ice skating in Hell before she'll thank me.

"She shouldn't have been on him at all. A novice could wreck a horse like that."

"You're welcome," I say as she snatches the reins from Drake. "Happy to help."

"I hardly think Amber's a novice," Drake says. He's regarding me now, a long, searching look from those deep brown eyes and one which makes me feel shaky. I stare back at him and my heart thuds like Chances' hooves on the damp earth. "No novice would be able to ride that horse at a walk, let alone jump him over a five bar gate."

Emily snorts rudely.

"All gyppos can stick on, Drake. It's what they do," she says nastily and with this charming parting shot stalks away, tugging Chances behind her by the bit ring. Drake winces but he doesn't say anything. What can he say? Chances is Emily's horse.

"Well?" I ask.

"Well what?"

"Isn't this the part where you tell me that she's all right really and didn't mean what she just said?"

He grimaces. "Not today. That was unforgivably rude. The only thing I will say in her defence —"

"You're going to defend her?" I raise my eyes to the sky. Maybe I should dye my hair blonde next time? It seems to turn guys' brains to cream cheese.

"Let me finish, Rumplestiltskin," Drake says. "I was going to say that in her defence you've totally shown her up. Em's really struggling with Chances and seeing you ride up with him so chilled is a massive blow to her ego."

I don't comment but I think we can safely say Emily's ego is big enough to handle this.

51

"You've been keeping your talents very well hidden," Drake continues. He crosses his arms over his dark blue Ariat jacket and grins. "Well, it's no use pretending you only ride a bit now. I've seen what you can do and I'm impressed. There aren't many who can ride a horse like that. Like I told you before, he's talented but tricky. I'm not sure what the answer is."

"Really? I think the answer's obvious. Take the gadgets off and let him go forward," I say.

Drake nods thoughtfully. "You could be right but I don't think Emily will go for that somehow. She's all about control."

I open my mouth to say that she's a bully but shut it fast. Drake says Emily isn't his girlfriend but it's obvious he fancies her and her father pays his wages. After hearing Harry's story about how the Owen family lost their farm I totally get that Drake has to play a careful game. His eventing career depends on keeping Mal and Emily sweet.

"So now your secret's out and this time I'm not taking no for an answer," Drake adds.

"Answer to what?"

"You coming to work for me. An hour every evening after school and all day at the weekends. What do you say? I need somebody with guts to help bring on my youngsters and from what I've seen today you're just the girl for the job. You've got talent too."

For a second excitement rises in me like a hot air balloon let off a string before it comes crashing back down.

"I don't think Emily will like that much."

"It's not Emily's decision," Drake says firmly. "I run this yard and my eventers my way and I hire people I believe can do the job. I'm warning you, there'll be a lot of mucking out and chores to get through before you're allowed anywhere near a horse. So, Rumplestiltskin, what do you say?"

Three weeks ago I was living on the Shakespeare Estate, looking after Mum and hiding from the bailiffs. Drake Owen was just a name from magazines and a face smiling out at me from the shelves of the local newsagent's. Now he's standing opposite me, male model gorgeous in cream breeches and black boots, telling me I've got talent and offering me a job on his yard.

I feel like pinching myself.

"Well?" he asks, holding out his hand, I reach out my own and smile. "What do you say?"

"I say yes," I tell him.

A job at Drake's yard means I can save money up for Mum, pay for Scally and even help Kate a little too. But most of all it means I'll get to see Chances every day and make his life a little more bearable.

There was only ever one answer really, wasn't there?

CHAPTER 9

It's another glorious autumnal day and the sunshine is streaming in through the classroom window. While the other students amuse themselves by playing on their mobiles or throwing things around the room I'm busy sketching Chances. Now and again I glance outside and dream about leaping onto his back, jumping the tatty playground fence to gallop over the hills and far far away. God, I wish I could do that. I've not ridden him again but the memory of the way Chances leapt the five bar gate and the ease of that stride as it covered the ground has stayed with me. I relive it far more than I probably should do, usually when I'm mucking out or scrubbing buckets, and I'm living for the time when it might happen again.

Hmm. That's as likely right now as me getting an A grade on this science essay I'm supposed to be writing. There's no way I can concentrate with all the din going on in the classroom. The teacher is engrossed in her laptop – she's probably on Facebook – and shows no sign of looking up and attempting to control the class. Not that she could if she tried. A lion tamer would struggle with this bunch. It takes all my will power not to leave my seat and slip out of the room. Only my promise to Harry and the fact that I'm enjoying working at the stables keeps me sitting down.

I shade a little more of Chances' mane and narrow my eyes critically. I know I'm good at drawing but even so I can't capture his energy and grace any more than Emily can ride him properly. I've only been working at the Rectory Stables for a few evenings but already I've watched enough of her training sessions to know even if she schools him for a million years she will never, ever get Chances to do things her way. It's painful to watch her pull and yank him around and I've been glad that I've got seven stables to muck out to distract me from having to witness too much. Seeing Drake ride is a totally different experience. Emily is good, I can't stand her but I can see that she's determined and skilled in a brutal kind of way, but

Drake's in a different league altogether. When he rides it's like watching ballet as the horses float across the arena as supple as dancers and pop four foot jumps as easily as trotting poles. While I scrub buckets and wash the cobbles with Jeyes fluid (my new and very sexy perfume) I learn so much just from watching him.

Emily wasn't thrilled to find me on her yard but Drake must have made it plain that this was his decision and so far she's left me alone – although she makes sure I have the grottiest chores and never misses an opportunity to point out that I'm basically her servant. I've put up with a lot worse though and this is a small price to pay in order to be near horses and have the chance learn to more about stable management. Emily might ride her string of glossy horses and have lessons but I'm learning too. Drake's taught me to bandage and poultice and I'm picking up what the action of certain bits may be. Compared to helping out at the riding school this is like getting out of a spitfire and into a space ship. If I never even get to sit on a horse at least I'm around them again.

Harry's reaction regarding my new job was predictable. He shot me a black look, stomped out of the farm house and hasn't spoken to me since. He's made it clear that he thinks I'm a traitor.

"It's a good job," I'd said to Kate. "I'll be able to send the neighbours some money for Scally and help Mum when I get home. I had three jobs in Bristol and I've lost them all. I have to do something."

Hands covered in flour from kneading bread at the table, Kate paused mid task and nodded.

"He'll calm down, love, and then you can explain it to him. He'll understand."

Somehow I doubted this. Harry hated the Owens and I couldn't imagine what I could possibly say that would make him understand why I'd want to work for Drake.

"He's still hurting so much about his dad," Kate continued quietly. "It's been so hard for him, Amber. He and Ben were very close. He needs someone to blame in order to make sense of it all but there are just some things that just don't make much sense at all, aren't there?"

I'd nodded. Mum's illness doesn't make sense to me. When she goes into that dark place where I can't reach her, for instance, or when they tell me I'm too young to understand, as though getting older makes people any wiser. They're just wrinkly and confused then, as far as I can see. They don't seem to know any more than I do.

I'd found Harry in his workshop. A harrow was on the ground and he was busy welding something to it, sparks fantailing into the air and making him glow crimson. Or maybe that was down to his mood?

Catching sight of me, he paused and pushed his mask up into his thick blonde hair.

"What?"

"You know what," I said. "The job."

Harry turned his back on me and started whacking a hammer against the harrow. I hoped it wasn't a voodoo hammer.

"Why are you asking me? Thought you'd already taken it."

Whack! Whack! Whack! Went the hammer and I flinched with every blow.

"I'd like to. No, it's more than that. I need to."

"So you can hang out with golden boy?" The scorn in his words was hotter than the molten metal.

"Don't be so childish! I need the money."

Harry snorted rudely. "What for? Hair dye?"

These comments stung. I knew my red hair was coming back with a vengeance but quite frankly that was the least of my concerns.

"To send back to our neighbour. Scally's costing too much to feed and Lynn can't keep her without money." There was a knot in my throat and I just about managed to choke out the rest. "She'll have to go to the rescue shelter otherwise and then ..."

My words petered out. I didn't need to fill in the blanks and the tears that I had held back for so long decided this was it it. Harry dropped his hammer and folded me into a hug while I hiccupped and sniffed and blubbed all over his overalls. He didn't say a word, none of the usual platitudes about how it would be all right in the end or not to worry, but instead let me sob until I was all cried out. He smelt of soap and hay and burned metal and being held by him felt nice.

It felt safe.

I wasn't used to feeling safe. Most of the time I feel as though I'm in a lift and descending very fast. Shaken, I placed my palms against his chest and gently stepped away.

"Sorry. I don't know where that came from."

"Don't you?"

I wiped my nose and eyes with my cuff.

"Maybe."

"Your Mum's in hospital and you haven't seen her for weeks, you've been dumped miles from home with a quite frankly dysfunctional family, you're having a crap time at school, you're worried about your home and now you're trying to work out how to stop your dog going to the pound." Harry ticked each of these off on his fingers. "They make quite an alarming list. I'm not surprised you're upset."

"I have to find a way to keep Scally safe," I said. "If I can send money back then I think Lyn would keep her for a bit longer. Until I get back anyway."

Harry said quietly, "Have you any idea how long that could be?"

Actually I had. I'd the pleasure of attending a core group meeting earlier and the upshot seemed to be that I'd be staying in Cornwall for a while yet. My new social worker, a caring beardy guy in a purple smock called Alan, had promised to drive me to Bristol to visit Mum but nothing had been said about returning permanently.

I swallowed back my misery. "A while I think."

Certainly far too long for Lynn who, fat and smoking forty a day, was tired of chasing after a lively dog.

Harry said quietly. "Look, my issues with Drake are nothing to do with you. You like horses and you like Drake – I can see that I'm not a total idiot – and you need the money too. It's a no brainer. Take the job."

"You mean it?"

"Yes. I work for Michael and he employs Drake. If I was really so highly principled I wouldn't work for him, would I? But we need the money here and you need the money for Scally."

"And Mum. She's got a few debts," I admitted.

I hadn't told him everything. For example, I didn't tell him about the bailiffs or the electric getting cut off. Some things I keep to myself because I never want to betray Mum. She's tried her best, it's just that things get on top of her at times. Incredibly, Harry was more than understanding. He got what it was like to feel responsible for a parent and to do your best to protect them.

"No more riding wild horses, though?" he'd warned and I'd agreed, crossing my fingers behind my back. In reality I was living for the next time I rode Chances. Besides, the Arab wasn't wild. He was just misunderstood.

Anyway, Harry's cool with my job which is a relief. I should have a few pounds by the weekend which I can send to Lynn and in a couple of weeks I'll have saved enough to square up the phone bill too. I can tell Mum all about it when I see her and hopefully this will cheer her up. I might be miles away but at least I can still help.

The bell rings and there's a stampede out of the classroom. The teacher doesn't even look up. I put my drawing away and weave my way around knocked down chairs and splayed text books. Freedom beckons, or at least my version of it which involves mucking out seven stables and trundling barrow loads of manure around. At this rate my muscles will have muscles.

The bus ride back to St Perran passes quietly enough. I text Lynn to ask about Scally but there's no answer. I'm not sure if that's good or bad and by the time I reach the Rectory I've gnawed the skin on my right thumb so much it's bleeding. Very attractive, Amber.

I hoist my school bag onto my shoulder and trudge up the drive to the yard. The bus goes practically via John O' Groats to get back and by the time I arrive Emily, who has a lift home, is already in the and school warming up on Chances. Drake stands in the middle with wrap around shades shielding his eyes but I can tell by the stiff set of his shoulders and the way his teeth worry his bottom lip that he's on edge.

"Circle again!" I hear him call. "More inside leg! Push him into the contact! Soften! Soften! If you pull against him it's not going to work."

I know I have the mucking out to do and that tack cleaning's also on my agenda tonight but I can't help myself; I have to watch. Chances is cantering around the school like a crab, snatching at the reins and throwing up his head, and Emily's face is set in a grimace as she tries her best to steady him.

"Inside leg!" Drake shouts. "Ride him forwards! Don't pull him back!"

But I can see Emily can't do this. Her hands are set and she daren't let the horse flow forward in the way he needs. The raw power that thrills me unnerves her and Emily's every instinct is telling her to hold and gather. Some horses might respond to this but not Chances. The tighter her grip and the more tense she becomes, the more upset he grows. With every lap of the school he winds up a little more until they are cantering sideways.

"Downwards transitions," Drake orders. "We need to break this cycle and get him focused."

This is a smart idea. Taking Chances back to basics and schooling him quietly in some circles and serpentines will defuse him and take his mind away from the excitement of jumping. If Emily carries on like this, it's going to end in disaster.

But Emily isn't impressed.

"I'm going to take him over the jumps," she calls back. "He needs to know who's boss and get working."

Drake doesn't even have a chance to reply before she whips Chances around on his hocks and heads for the first jump. The speed is breathtakingly fast and they fly over in a chestnut blur and land with a flurry of sand and rubber shreds. The second jump is taken with equal speed and the third too. By the time Emily turns for the fourth Chances has stretched into a flat out gallop down the long side.

"Steady him!" Drake yells, but Emily either can't hear or she can't collect the Arab. Either way they approach the combination way too fast and Chances, his head held too tightly to stretch out, ploughs straight through. Poles fly across the school like match sticks and as Emily lurches forward the horse snatches the reins in a bid for freedom and explodes in a series of bucks. Emily loses both her stirrups and for a few stomach lurching seconds it looks as though she's about to fall.

Drake has drained of colour and my heart is racing. As the Arab tears around the arena we're seeing broken necks and legs, both equine and human. Somehow Emily manages to stick on and after several circuits pulls Chances up. As the horse stands, flanks heaving and nostrils flared, she raises her crop and brings it down on his flank with all her might. Once, twice and then for a third time.

I can't help myself. I'm ducking through the fence and running towards her before my brain's registered what I'm doing. As Emily brings her crop down again I managed to grab her wrist and block the blow.

"Get out of my way," she snarls.

My left hand curls around the reins while my right soothes Chances' neck. I feel the horse tremble and I'm so angry I can hardly speak.

"No," I say. "Not until you get off."

"Take your hand off my horse," Emily hisses. Her blue eyes are narrowed with rage. "He's got to learn."

"Not like this!"

"He needs to know who's in charge! And he's not the only one. Haven't you got some mucking out to do? That's what my father pays you for." She yanks the whip out of my grasp and brandishes it. "Now move, skank."

"Get off the horse." Drake is at my side. His hand covers mine on the reins and for a moment I think he's squeezing my fingers before I realise that he's actually taking hold of the horse. Feeling foolish, I slide mine away.

"What?" Emily says.

"Get off. Now." Drake's voice is brittle with anger. "You heard me. Off."

Emily opens her mouth to protest but Drake's expression silences her. Looking mutinous she swings her right leg over Chances' neck and jumps to the ground.

"He needs to learn his lesson," she mutters sulkily.

"Chances hasn't done anything wrong. That was all your doing. If you want to blame anyone, then you don't have much further to look than yourself. And as for losing your temper? You should be ashamed of yourself," Drake tells her.

Emily's mouth falls open. I can't imagine anyone's ever spoken to her like that before.

"He's my horse and I can do what I like!"

"Not on my watch," Drake says. "If you want to behave like a ham fisted pony club brat then be my guest but I won't be training you. Come back when you're in the mood to actually listen and if you're not, then don't come back at all. Find yourself another trainer."

Emily glares at him but there's steel in Drake's voice and she thinks better of arguing. Instead, she shoots me an evil and stalks away. Great. School will be even worse tomorrow. Something I would have said earlier was impossible.

Drake turns to me.

"Take Chances back. Wash him down, cool him off and turn him. I'll tack up Nightshade."

I love watching Drake schooling. Coal black Nightshade is his top horse and they're a dream team. Maybe if I'm quick with my mucking out I can watch?

"You're riding?"

"Nope," Drake replies. "You are. It's high time you were back in the saddle and I seem to have a spare hour on my hands all of a sudden. Are you up for it?"

Up for it? A lesson on a top horse with one of Britain's best event riders? Am I ever.

It certainly beats mucking out.

CHAPTER 10

"You look happy, love," Kate comments when I arrive back at the farmhouse that evening. She's at the Aga frying something spicy that makes my mouth water and she smiles warmly. "Did you have a good time at the yard?"

I must usually look a right misery if several hours of mucking out and a further forty minutes of being hollered at by Drake has put a smile on my face. I thought I could ride but endless circuits of the sand school being bawled at soon put me straight on that score. Nightshade's fluid movement fell apart as soon as I was in the saddle and I've never had to work so hard to keep a horse in an outline or moving straight. My stomach and legs are in agony, my head's spinning from all Drake's instructions and I stink of horse but actually she's right; I am happy. For the first time since I arrived here I've not been thinking about Mum or how I can get home to care for her but have actually focused on something else.

I feel really guilty.

"It was all right," I mutter.

"I wasn't criticising. Being happy is a good thing," Kate clarifies hastily. "There's nothing wrong with being happy, Amber. That is allowed."

"Even we still feel happy and our dad's dead," Maddy points out. She's sitting at the table, supposedly doing her homework but actually reading the latest Jaqueline Wilson. She's living with the real deal, I think as I pull off my boots and join her. Mad mums. Sink estates. In trouble at school. The list goes on and on. If only my life had a funky cover and a happy ending. Wouldn't that be nice?

Kate winces.

"I don't think that comment helps much, Mads. Everyone's circumstances are different."

"But Amber's mum *is* alive even if she is in hospital," Maddy points out with faultless logic. "She'll see her again soon but we'll never…never…"

Her words fade and her bottom lip starts to wobble. Saffy pads over and rests her head on Maddy's knee. Maddy buries her face in the dark fur and her shoulders shake.

Kate looks at me helplessly. The pan's sizzling and she stirs like mad to stop the food catching. I put my arm around Maddy and give her a hug.

"You're right. I'm lucky because I will see Mum again at some point."

How can I explain to that sometimes it feels just like my mum has died? The mum I love, the one who liked to bake and walk Scally and play the guitar, that mum went away a long time ago and I don't know if I'll ever see her again. The sad faced stranger in her place looks like her but she's really not the same person. Dogood says Mum will get better and it's just a matter of finding the right medicine but I'm not convinced. In four years they haven't found it yet, have they?

"But you're not going yet?" Maddy looks up and there's a note of panic in her voice. "Not for ages. We'll still go to school on the bus together, won't we?"

Maddy's still having a hard time at school. It's not much fun for either of us but it's worse for her because at least I can leave whereas she's only in Year Seven and has ages to go. On the bright side at least Emily will leave in May but I know that's not much comfort when you're eleven and six months feels like six years.

To be honest it feels that way when you're fifteen too. I'm still counting the days until I manage to go home and my heart twists for Maddy.

"Of course we will," I promise. "My mum's still poorly. You can't get rid of me that easily."

Maddy looks more cheerful and returns to orphans/dustbin babies/Victorian scullery maids. Kate gives me a grateful look and I feel warm all over. It's hard work being disliked and this makes a nice change. I can't risk getting too close though because that will make leaving hard when the time comes. It's my cardinal rule and I'm quite alarmed how close I'm starting to get to breaking it.

Take Chances for instance. Try as I might I can't put him out of my mind. Every night I drift off to sleep reliving our gallop through the woods and feeling the power beneath me as his muscles coiled before he sprung over the gate. Seeing him yanked about by Emily is unbearable and if I can make his life easier in any small ways while I'm at the yard then that's what I'll do. After my yard chores were done I wandered down to the paddock and gave him a handful of pony nuts and a scratch behind the ears. He whickered when he saw me and trotted over with that magical floating gait that hardly seems to touch the grass. He was in disgrace after the incident with Emily and Drake, joining me at the gate, was far too professional to criticize but I could tell he was losing patience.

"If things don't improve soon I can't see Emily keeping Chances. He's not going to win the big classes she's got her heart set on," Drake confided, leaning across and running his tanned hand down the Arab's neck.

"He could easily win," I'd said, stung on Chances' behalf. "He's a fantastic horse and he jumps like he's got wings. And his paces are gorgeous. He'd wipe the floor in the dressage."

"With his turn of speed he's incredible in a jump off," Drake sighed. "He's got it all but he's a tricky one but we knew that when he bought him. A horse like Chances could go either way."

"But he's amazing. Can't you ride him?"

He shook his head. "I'm too heavy. Besides, I've got enough on with my own horses and Chances belongs to Mike who'll only see him as a business expense to move on."

I'd only met Michael Lacey once. A red faced man wearing beige cords and a check coat he'd seemed pleasant enough as he'd chatted to Drake about Emily's progress but it didn't strike me that he knew much about horses. I supposed he didn't have to though, all he needed to do was sign the cheques.

"The trouble is, Em won't want to put the time in," Drake sighed. "She's got talent but she doesn't want to work at it and horses like Chances needs consistent schooling to build a relationship. He needs to trust his rider. Things go badly wrong and fast for a horse like him otherwise."

My stomach lurched. If Chances didn't behave Emily would sell him on. Drake's meaning was clear; Chances' future was bleak if he didn't settle down. I had to do something to help him.

I *had* to.

Recalling this conversation, I make a decision. It's not one Drake will approve of, Harry certainly won't like it and Kate, if she ever finds out, will totally freak but I don't think I have any choice. If I don't help Chances then he'll hurt himself or Emily or both of them so I'm going to school him myself.

I know. It's mad, but since being mad runs in the family that's my excuse. The truth is I know I can ride Chances and I know I can help him too. The really crazy thing is to stand back and do nothing.

"Dinner won't be for a while," Kate straightens up from placing a large casserole dish in the Aga. "Harry's not due home for another hour. He's just called and said he's driving past Exeter."

Maddy looks up in surprise. "Why's he in Exeter?"

"He's been out," her mother replies. We both wait for an explanation but Kate turns her attention to rinsing a saucepan and any questions we might have won't be heard anyway above the clatter of cast iron pots.

"Harry never goes anywhere," Maddy says, puzzled.

It's true. Harry is tied to the farm. If he isn't ploughing or planting or doing things with the stinky muck spreader he's crashed out on the sofa or shoveling up huge amounts of food. I think he's visited to the local town once since I've been here but I could be wrong.

"Maybe he's met a girl. On the Internet?" Maddy continues, her eyes wide.

I think this highly unlikely. Harry wouldn't be interested in meeting girls. He's far too busy. Whenever I catch him browsing he's drooling over tractors, not Tinder.

Still. Not my business. Harry can do whatever he likes and while Kate continues to clatter and Maddy returns to her homework, I slip out the back door. My homework will have to fester in the bottom of my bag for a bit longer because I have far more important things to do.

The farm yard must have been beautiful in its hey day. There are cobbles, big stone barns with enormous timber frames and a row of stables where once upon a time cart horses must have tugged at hay nets. Now these house Harry's tractor and trailer as well as a load of other farm yard stuff I don't have a clue about and gangly weeds poke through the cobbles. Nobody here as time to tend the yard; they're all far too busy worrying about making ends meet, I get that now, and I do feel guilty about the nasty comments I made when I first arrived.

At the end of the stable block is an old harness room where tarnished brasses hang from rusting nails and cobwebs are draped over tack that's grown stiff with age and neglect. Like a lot of things at Perranview Farm this must have all been totally amazing in it's hey day but now it feels sad and lonely and rather unloved.

I've only been inside the old harness room once when Maddy showed me the old buildings. It was dark and dusty so we hadn't stayed long but it was enough time for me to notice an array of bits and bridles lined up on pegs. Somewhere in here I know I'll find something that will fit Chances. With the saddle soap I've borrowed from the Rectory and a bit of hard work I'll have something that should work. I'll have to ride bareback but I'll take the risk. I used to ride bareback all the time when I helped at the riding school.

The light in the harness room is dim and the electricity has been long disconnected so it takes a while for my eyes to adjust. When they do I soon find what I'm looking for – a simple cavesson bridle with plaited leather reins and a very grubby snaffle. Chances' bit is expensive, golden and gleaming, so this will be a bit of a come down. On the other hand, at least I won't haul him about like Emily and with a bit of elbow grease I can make this bit as good as new. Tack cleaning's something I'm getting very good at since I started working for Drake.

I unhook the bridle. The leather feels hard and brittle beneath my finger tips. I wonder how long it is since it was last cleaned? And who did it belong to? Not the farmer's cob or one of the plough horses, that's for sure because it's far too small. I suppose it belonged to a pony or small horse, perhaps belonging to the children, and long since forgotten. For some reason this thought makes me feel really sad.

Bridle firmly in my grasp, I retreat to my room on the pretext of doing some homework but in reality to fill the sink with warm water and soap the hard leather until my fingers turn all wrinkly. I lay the pieces out on a towel and then turn my attention to the bit, soaking it in a mug full of hot water until all the grime and dried on grass fall away. Then I buff it with my tasseled scarf until it gleams, my fingers tingle and I've got a shiny loose ring snaffle. I'm just about to make a start on oiling the leather when there's thudding of paws up the attic stairs, followed by the scrabbling of claws and whining.

"Hold on, Saffy," I call, wiping my hands dry on my school trousers and laying the brow band alongside the cheek pieces. I open the door but rather than a solid mass of black fur hurling itself my legs I'm greeted by a bouncing ball of white and ginger fluff.

It's my dog, Scally.

No way. It can't be!

Scally barks and barks before leaping into my arms and covering my face in wet doggy kisses.

"What are you doing here?" I ask, squeezing her tightly and burying my face in her wiry coat. "How on earth did you find me?"

Then the penny drops. Harry went to fetch her. That's why he's been gone all day on a mysterious errand and why he was driving back along the motorway earlier. Harry went all the way to Bristol to find Scally. He listened when I told him how worried I was about her but more than that – he's actually done something to make it right.

This has to be the nicest thing anyone has ever done for me.

Still hugging Scally, I fly down the stairs and burst into the kitchen where I find Harry and Kate looking very smug.

"Surprised?" Harry asks.

"I don't know what to say."

"You don't need to say anything," he grins. "The look on your face says it all. I'm glad you're pleased."

"I'm more than pleased! I'm over the moon!" I gently lower Scally to the floor and instantly Saffy and the cat come over to say hello. While they sniff and wag their tails and hiss, depending on species, I pat her head and do my best to get control of my emotions.

"She's really pleased to see you. As soon as Harry arrived she knew you were here. She jumped out of his arms and raced up the stairs," Kate remarks. "She's a very clever dog, Amber."

"I know." I'm still unable to speak much.

"Is she living here now?" Maddy wants to know. She crouches down next to Scally and strokes her, laughing delightedly when my dog rolls over to have her tummy tickled.

"Of course. Scally is welcome to stay here for as long as Amber does," Kate replies.

"She'll love it here," Maddy says. There's a determined expression on her face. "I expect she'll want to stay forever."

Kate lays a gentle hand on her daughter's shoulder. "Amber's only here for a while, love. She will go home again at some point."

Home. That reminds me. Harry's been to the Shakespeare Estate. In his country boots and waxed jacket he must have stood out a mile. In fact, he's lucky to make it out alive.

I hope he wasn't mugged.

"How was Lynn? Did she mind you taking Scally?" I ask.

"Your neighbour's an interesting lady." Harry leans against the Aga, arms crossed over his plaid shirt, and winks. "Let's say she didn't seem the type who'd walk a dog."

"The furthest Lynn goes is to the fridge," I say.

"No wonder she was so happy to let me take Scally," he grins. "I had to leave a contribution towards her expenses though. What on earth does your dog eat? Fillet steak? Thirty quid's worth?"

He *has* been mugged.

"I'll pay you back," I promise. I'll clean twice as much tack, muck out twenty stables, take all the abuse Emily throws at me if it means I can repay Harry.

"Don't be daft. I wanted to do it. It's worth every penny not to see your usual sulky glower. Puts me right off my food, seeing that across the table every meal time."

"I can't say I'd noticed," I shoot back and he laughs.

"Talking of food," Kate says, "I've cooked a celebration curry to welcome Scally to Perranview. Maddy, get some plates from the dresser for us, please, and I'll dish up."

As Maddy sets the table, Harry joins me and pats Scally. She likes him and jumps into his arms, licking his chin and barking.

"You're a bit lighter than Saffy," he remarks. "Maybe you can ride in the tractor while your mum's at school. Would you like that?"

Scally barks.

"I'll take that as a yes," Harry says.

"Thank you," I say. "I don't know why you did that, but thank you. It was really kind."

"That's what friends do, Amber. They're kind to each other. Not everyone's out to get you, you know," he says quietly.

I think the jury's still out there but as we sit at the table I can't help thinking I've never in my whole life had a friend as kind as Harry Crewe.

And hold on. Harry says he's my friend. How on earth has that happened?

I'm not sure what's changed but something has. The spiky feeling I usually have when I'm with Harry isn't there anymore. Instead I feel warm and safe and happy.

It's weird.

And it's also very, very nice.

CHAPTER 11

It's ridiculous how much noise a house makes at night. I'm sure in the day time the stairs don't creak so loudly or the hinges on the kitchen door groan as much. Even my socked feet echo when I pad across the flagstones. Just as well Saffy and Scally are in the boot room because they'd have given the game away for sure. The last thing I need is Kate catching me in the act. Fully dressed and clutching a bridle in my hands, I don't think the excuse that I'm thirsty would have worked.

Luckily for me everyone else is sleeping soundly. Harry's exhausted from the drive to Bristol and I hold my breath as I tiptoe past his door because he'd know in a heart beat exactly what I'm up to. It's freaky with Harry; it's like he can read my mind and knows exactly what I'm planning almost before I know myself. I've got nowhere to go if he's in my head!

I'm still reeling from the kindness of his driving all the way to Bristol to bring Scally back for me. I still don't really understand why he did it. I've been nothing but trouble for him and Kate since I arrived and *project get sent home* must have given them a fair few headaches. I feel like the world's turned upside down. Things I thought were true maybe aren't and things I thought I wanted I'm not so sure about anymore. I mean, I of course I want to go home to to Mum but I'm also starting to like it here too. Am I being disloyal?

My head starts to ache so I shove all these worries aside and step outside. It's a beautiful clear night with the moon smiling over the orchard and the dark sky sprinkled with stars. As I walk down the lane to the stables I hear owls calling, the distant bark of a fox and the world seems full of possibilities.

The paddock is silvered by the moonlight and a dark shape at the far side shifts at my approach.

"Chances!" I call softly as I climb the fence.

There's whicker in reply and a shadow breaks into a canter. Seconds later Chances buries his soft muzzle in the pony nuts I've crammed into my pockets. I loop the reins over his neck, slip the bit into his mouth and the head piece over his ears. Once the throat lash is buckled I slide across from the fence onto Chances' warm back.

"Ready to ride?" I whisper.

It's lucky for me that it's a moonlit night because otherwise it would be hard to see. The paddock is roughly a square in shape and in my mind's eye I work out a school. C is up there by the oak tree and A is right down by the fence. It's all a bit wonky and we're on a bit of a slope but as I walk Chances around on a loose rein I pick out where I think the other markers might be. I've watched Drake and Emily schooling for long enough to have memorized the positions and I can remember some of the exercises I used to do at the riding school. There are circles and serpentines and leg yields to do and maybe some counter canter and figures of eight too. I know Chances can do it all. I just hope I'm good enough to do him justice.

I push him into a trot and for the first couple of laps it takes all my concentration to stay on. Chances shies and tries to run away with me like he does with Emily but I've seen enough of their pulling war to know I must soften my hands and use my stomach and shoulders to slow the gait. By the time he's going nicely and in something resembling an outline my stomach muscles are screaming. I grit my teeth and ask for canter. At the very least I'll have ripped abs after all this!

Chances' canter is as bouncy as a rubber ball and the power in his stride makes my heart swell as we circle and do figures of eight. I feel the Arab settle beneath me and start to focus on his work, accepting the bit and pushing forwards with his hind quarters. The reins are elastic in my hands and his mouth peachy soft as he takes the contact. I'm no expert on dressage but I'm sure this is good, good enough even for a three-day-event…

All of a sudden there's a rustle in the trees and Chances spooks sharply. Deep in day dreams of competing at Badminton my concentration isn't on the horse beneath me and before I know it I'm on the floor while he kicks up his hooves and canters to the far side of the paddock. For a few minutes I lie on my back looking up at the stars and gasping, before horrible images of caught reins and sore mouths galvanize me to limp across the paddock and catch him.

Chances is cropping the grass and doesn't seem any the worse for this. I check him over quickly and then take his bridle off. I think I'll quit while I'm ahead and still in one piece. I offer him a Polo which he takes with velvet soft lips.

"Same time tomorrow?" I ask.

In answer, Chances nudges the crook of my arm which might mean yes or might mean more Polos. In any case, there's more of both. I'm really pleased with our evening's schooling. Chances has proved beyond all doubt that he can go nicely and hopefully he'll remember some of this next time Emily rides him. Just imagine what he could do in a proper arena and with a saddle! I feel almost dizzy with excitement.

Still, all that's a while away and even if it does happen I don't suppose I'll be the girl in the saddle. Real life doesn't work like that. I scratch the horse's neck under the mane in the place I know he likes and then I leave him in the darkness. It's nice to dream.

"You look very pale, love," Kate remarks a few days later. "Do you feel all right? Or do you think you're coming down with something?"

It's early on Saturday morning and I'm slumped at the kitchen table, doing my best not to fall asleep face first in my bowl of porridge. I'm working all day at the stables, no doubt Emily will have thought of some really great chores for me like scrubbing stable matts or unblocking drains, and I'm trying to keep my eyes open. I've ridden Chances every night this week and the lack of sleep is getting to me. I fell asleep in registration yesterday which gave Emily the opportunity to hide my bag and make me late for my first lesson. I picked up a detention and then another when I fell asleep in French. The only thing that kept me from losing the plot was the secret knowledge that the previous night Chances had cantered perfect figures of eight with flying changes and had executed a beautiful half pass too. We'd even jumped the paddock post and rails four times, Chances flying over the fence easily. When Emily had ridden him earlier he'd raced around the school with a hollow back and his nose poked in the air. Even the draw reins she insisted on were hardly working and, knowing just how beautifully he could go in a simple snaffle and without a martingale, I could hardly bear to watch.

I smother a yawn. "I'm just a bit tired."

"Tired? I've seen pandas with less black around their eyes."

This comment's from Harry who's popped in for a bacon sandwich. Narrowing his eyes suspiciously, he adds, "What are you up to, Amber? Sneaking out all night to go partying?"

"In my dreams," I say, although he's not as far from the truth as he thinks. "It's not exactly party central here, is it?"

"St Perran is a bit quiet," Kate agrees. "I hope you're not too bored, love?"

Bored? Hardly. When I'm not being Emily's slave I'm being barked at by Drake while I ride his horses or I'm doing chores around the farm. Then I'm riding Chances in the small hours and trying to catch up on my homework. Chuck a few meetings with Caring Alan into the mix and writing to Mum and you can safely say I'm not bored.

"It's fine," is all I say and Harry rolls his eyes.

"Glad we pass the Amber Evans approval test," he says.

I put my spoon down and push the bowl aside. I'm too exhausted to even eat. When I get to the stables I'll make a strong coffee to ping me awake. Kate doesn't stock Red Bull, my Bristol breakfast of choice, so I'm developing an addiction to Drake's Nesspresso machine. That would make Mum laugh. She's longed for one of those ever since she saw the advert with George Clooney. I'm not sure if she actually thinks George comes with the coffee maker though; it's hard to tell with her sometimes.

I think I could walk to the stables with my eyes shut and I practically do this morning since I'm so tired. It's another beautiful autumnal day and the leaves are russet and orange and scarlet while the sea in the dip between the valley turns to liquid gold in the sunshine. Scally bounces along in front of me, barking excitedly at falling leaves and tearing off as she picks up rabbit scents. She's loving it here. Of course she is. Woody tracks and ploughed up fields are a billion time better than the litter strewn streets of the Shakespeare Estate.

Oh no. I'm doing it again, aren't I? Thinking that it's nicer here than at home…

Ok, I admit it. It is nicer here. I do like it. I even think sometimes I might be happier in a weird kind of way but I mustn't think like that because I'll have to go back at some point. Bristol is home and Mum needs me and it's as simple as that. I ought to know by now that there's absolutely no point growing fond of the foster families I stay with.

"You're late," says Drake when I walk into the yard. He glances at the big event watch he always wears on his tanned wrist. "Ten minutes, late."

"Sorry," I say, shutting Scally into a stable. "I overslept."

"Out partying?"

Why do people keep saying that? My hair's a state, I've no time to bother with makeup and I'm exhausted. Hardly party animal material.

"Your hair? You've done something to it?" Drake reaches out and brushes curls out of my face. "Coloured it? Curled it? For a date? It suits you."

My hair is red again and it's wild and shaggy too. The black dye was a wash in fade out job and it's totally given up. I'm ginger, as Emily and her cronies like to snigger, and without my makeup I'm paler than one of Stephanie Meyer's vampires – appropriate seeing as I feel like the undead most mornings.

"I'm way too busy for dates or parties. Sorry for being late. Where do you want me to start?"

Drake gives me his brown eyed smile and the hairs on my forearms ripple. Why do I feel there's another conversation going on here? A sub text I can't quite pick up on?

"Since you working it'd better be something to do horses," he says softly.

I don't speak. For a second the air feels all static and weird. Why do have the feeling there's something else he wants to say? I'm just on the brink of asking him what's up when he exhales and shakes his head as though trying to dislodge the words he was searching for.

"I've tacked up Jet. Time to take him over the jumps."

"Seriously?"

Drake's been bawling me out all week about my riding. It's all hands this, leg that and shoulders back the other. I haven't glimpsed so much as a trotting pole. In fact, if it wasn't for my secret late night schooling sessions I'd be thinking I was crap and tempted to give up.

"Seriously. Look, Amber, I know I've given you a hard time but I needed to see if you have what it takes to make it. If you think you're perfect and aren't prepared to work, then you can have all the talent in the world but you'll never succeed in eventing. I've been watching you ride and I can see you've really listened to me. You've got talent and determination and a work ethic. Those are the very things things you need to make it in our game."

It's the way he says *our game* as much as the unexpected praise, that makes me feel warm all over. I'm part of something and maybe I could be something too? I tingle with possibilities.

Drake legs me up and tightens my girth. Then he opens the gate to the school and watches me work Jet in, calling out instructions. A course of jumps has set up already, nothing higher than three feet, and as I ride around them I imagine how it's going to feel to fly over them.

Amazing, I think is the word.

Jet is one of Drake's youngsters. A Dutch warm blood of almost seventeen hands, he makes the jumps look tiny. He also needs a lot more leg to push him into my hands and by the time he's ready to jump I can hardly breathe.

"Fitness," Drake remarks dryly as I pause to get my breath and put up my stirrups, "isn't just something for the horse to worry about. If you're going to make it around a cross country course you need to be fit too. Time you started running and lifting some weights."

I laugh. "I lift enough buckets and rubber matts here and I'm always running over from the farm."

"It's not enough. You need a proper fitness routine," he says, deadly serious. "I run every morning at six. Why don't you join me?"

I roughly calculate that this will mean I'll have about four hours sleep a night and open my mouth to decline.

"OK, you're on."

What? What! Where did that come from? What on earth am I thinking? Apart from how much fun it could be to train with Drake and have him all to myself…

71

Now my face is really hot and I'm glad Drake can't read my mind, Harry style. At least he'll think it's the effort of riding Jet that's making my cheeks glow.

"What's she doing riding Jet? Have you flipped? He's your best hope for 2020!"

Emily leans on the gate and her pretty face is twisted into an expression that looks oddly like envy. Chances, trussed up in leather like something from a dodgy late night cable TV channel, is standing beside her. Already I can see the white of his eyes and sense his growing agitation.

"Amber's popping him around the jumps," Drake says evenly. "It's good for him to have a different jockey on board and good for me to see him move from the ground. Already I can see he's coming up short on the near hind."

But Emily couldn't give a hoot about the theory.

"She'll wreck him. For God's sake, Drake. Let her get back to scrubbing buckets. I need the school anyway and you're paid to train me. Not her."

"It's not nine am yet. I'm on my time." Drake catches my eye and gives me a ghost of a wink. "Amber's pretty good and I'm thinking of letting her take Jet to the event at Colehydrack."

Emily scowls as she tows Chances, dancing and snorting, into the school.

"You're mad, Drake. She'll break her neck. Or even worse, his."

"It's nice of you to be so concerned, Emily, but I'll be fine," I say sweetly.

She makes a noise that's somewhere between a laugh and a snort, like a posh Peppa Pig.

"Anyone can jump Jet. He's brilliant. If you're so good why don't you try it on a difficult horse? If you can jump a round on this lunatic then maybe you're half way good enough to enter Colehydrack."

"Don't be ridiculous," Drake begins but stops because I've leapt off Jet, thrown the reins at him, vaulted onto Chances and am riding away to warm him up. Wow. A saddle! This is going to make life a whole bunch easier. Yippee!

"Amber, come back! This is crazy," I hear Drake call but this time I'm ignoring my trainer because unknowingly Emily has given me the perfect opportunity to do what I've been longing to – take Chances over a proper course rather than bits of old tree trunk and the paddock fence. Used to me after a week of midnight schooling, Chances relaxes through his paces and I feel him soften into the contact. I trot and canter on each rein just like in the paddock and then, because I can't resist it, make a figure of eight around the jumps and ask for a flying change.

"This is it boy," I whisper, winding my fingers into his mane and turning for the first fence. "Time to show them what you can do."

Chances' ears prick, he surges forward and we're over the first jump so easily that I hardly feel us leave the ground. Landing, I gather him for the next jump which he flies before turning for the combination and then an upright. The final jump is a spread and I know we'll have to approach with impulsion and control so I shift my weight a little to steady him as I half halt before letting him fly and cantering a lap of the school patting his neck and telling him how brilliant he is. Then I ask him to walk and he listens instantly, prancing and tossing his head because he knows how clever he is, but he's listening too. He's made it look easy and I think I'm going to explode with pride.

Drake's mouth is swinging open. It's just as well he hasn't any idea how I usually jump Chances and how many tumbles I've taken this week. It's certainly a whole lot easier with a saddle!

"I ought to say that was stupid and reckless," he scolds, "and it was, but it was also absolutely incredible. That's *exactly* the way Chances needs to be ridden. Tact and sympathy all the way with a horse like him. Brute force will never work."

"It was a fluke!" Emily, puce faced and seething, glowers at me from beneath the brim of her pink glittery riding hat. "The horse is coming good. It was bound to happen at some point. She's just lucky."

"She rode beautifully," Drake says quietly but Emily ignores him.

"Get off my horse, gyppo."

Reluctantly, I slide to the floor. Her insults wash right over me because I know just how much work it's taken to get this far. My head is buzzing with possibilities too as I imagine how good Chances and I could be. I know it's all dreams but I know we could jump the moon and the stars.

Emily hauls herself into the saddle and instantly Chances tenses and rolls his eyes. When he starts to dance her fingers close on the reins, making him snatch and pivot at the harsh contact.

"Right," she says through gritted teeth, "now watch how it's really done."

"Don't be so childish, Em! It's not a competition! Some horses just go better with some riders," Drake says evenly. "There's no shame in it. Event riders change horses all the time. It's not personal."

But to Emily it's very personal. She hates me and she hates that Drake thinks I might have a talent. It doesn't matter that all I've been given is just a little scrap compared to the opportunities lavished onto her. Even that's too much to bear. She jabs her spurred heels into Chances' sides and they shoot forwards towards the jumps.

It's too fast. Way, way too fast. Somehow they clear the first one and hurl themselves over the second before charging towards the combination. Chances' canter is no longer bouncy and rhythmic but disunited and ugly, the strides lengthening until he's galloping at the jump. I watch helplessly as

Emily saws at his mouth in an attempt to gain control.

"Slow down!" Drake yells but it's far too late. As Chances cat leaps the first element Emily wobbles and is left behind, losing her line to the second element and taking it at a slant. By the third jump they are so skew whiff that Chances sits right back on his hocks and leaps the wing, a jump that must be at least five feet.

It's too much for Emily. Already unbalanced and minus a stirrup, she pitches out of the saddle and falls into the jump with a sickening crack. Chances tears around the school, reins dangling and stirrups swinging, but there's no movement at all from his rider.

Emily Lacey lies motionless and crumpled amid the scattered poles.

CHAPTER 12

"It's probably just concussion but she'll need to be checked out. Hopefully nothing too serious, but you can never be too careful."

The paramedic's words are reassuring but Drake doesn't look convinced. The shock of seeing Emily unconscious and the drama of calling an ambulance has really shaken him.

"There's nothing broken?"

"Not as far as we can tell. She'll have an X ray on her arm but I'd put money on the fact it's just a sprain. You did everything exactly right. She's had a nasty tumble and she'll feel rough for a day or two but she'll be fine."

Emily is inside the ambulance with Michael. It's only the second time I've laid eyes on him but I'm impressed by how concerned he is for Emily. It's good to know that not all Dads push off when there's trouble.

"If you lot must sit on horses! Nasty beasts, dangerous at both ends," the paramedic adds when Drake fails to reply but even this attempt at humour fails to raise a smile.

Once the ambulance has left, Drake and I take the horses back to the yard. Neither of us feels like talking and it's only once the stable chores are done and the horses turned out that he comes to find me and delivers a mug of coffee. Taking it, I follow him into the sunshine and perch on the mounting block.

"I'd have put something stronger in it but you're too young," he teases.

"Where I come from they're necking cider by twelve," I reply, wrapping my cold fingers around the mug.

Drake gives me a sideways look. "Something tells me you're not joking."

I think about the Shakespeare Estate with its boarded up shops, graffiti and air of utter hopeless and I can't think of anything to laugh about.

"It's a bit different to here," is all I say. "Not many horses."

"So how come you're such a fantastic rider?"

"Fantastic? Me? I don't think so."

"Come on, Amber, let's not bother being modest. How the Hell you got Chances over the jumps like that is nothing short of a miracle. You're a natural horsewoman and you've got talent. We both know that if you were in Emily's shoes you'd be flying." He takes a sip of coffee and then says innocently, "It's almost like you've jumped Chances before."

I'm suddenly absolutely fascinated by the cobblestones. Hmm. They need a sweep.

"I'm not an idiot, Amber," Drake says. "And you don't always brush those bridle marks away as well as you think you do."

I look up, shocked.

"I know you've been riding him and I haven't said anything because…" he shakes his head as he searches for the words, "I guess because I like the horse and I like you too. You're both rebellious and spirited and independent and you make a good team. You're both talented too but when that talent isn't channeled there's trouble – as I imagine your teachers know."

My eyes are wide at this unexpected praise.

"But now, after seeing this display, I can't keep quiet anymore. There's no way you're to ride Chances, Amber. He's too volatile."

I round on him furiously. "But this wasn't his fault! You saw how beautifully he went with me! Emily can't ride a horse like Chances. You said so yourself, he needs patience and hard work and we both know she isn't big on either of those things."

"And the more she winds him up the worse he'll get," Drake agrees bleakly. He tips the dregs of his coffee onto the cobbles and I watch it sink into the cracks just like my hopes are sinking into despair. "After this I doubt Michael will want to keep him anyway."

A cold hand squeezes my heart. "You think they'd sell Chances?"

Drake nods. "Maybe it's for the best? He was always a gamble and it's clear it's not working out. If Michael asks my opinion I'm afraid I'm going to tell him I believe the horse should go."

"You don't mean that!"

His mouth is set in a grim line. "I do. This sport is deadly enough. I can't take any more risks."

I don't think I've ever felt so betrayed in all my life. Not even when Dad left. I could understand that, goodness knows I'd have left too if somebody had given me a choice, but I cannot understand how Drake could give up on Chances.

Unless of course this is more to do with how he feels about Emily?

Of course. It's so obvious. Drake's in love with Emily. Why has it taken me so long to see it? His loyalty is to her and Michael. All the big speeches about my talent and Chances' ability were just hot air.

I put my coffee cup down and walk across to the stable where Scally's snoozing.

"Come on, girl."

"Where are you going?" Drake asks.

"Anywhere but here." I'm not sticking around a second longer. Stuff his job. I can get a paper round or do some waitressing in one of the local pubs to earn some cash. Anything's better than this. I scoop my dog up in my arms and bury my face in her rough fur. It's a sad day when you realise that your dog really is the only person you can rely upon.

Drake stares at me. "Are you walking out on me?"

"Are you giving up on me?" I counter.

He fixes me with a look that stops me in my tracks. I can't move. I can hardly breathe.

"I'd never give up on you, Amber. Never. But whether or not you choose to believe that is up to you. But one thing I will tell you is that you won't be risking your neck on Chances. Absolutely no way. Not on my watch. You're way too important for that."

And with this comment, Drake walks away from me while I gaze after him with my heart racing.

What on earth was that all about?

I don't go to the stables on Sunday. Instead I mope about in my room and waste what's left of my mobile credit attempting to call Mum. The hospital won't put me through and in frustration I call Alan's off duty number and rage at him and demand to go home, prompting an emergency visit which sends Kate into a tail spin of cleaning and cake making. (*Chill*, I hear Harry say, *it's not as though he'll take Maddy away just because you haven't hoovered*) Over several cups of tea and half a coffee cake, most of which ends up in his beard, Alan finally agrees that he'll take me up to see my mother *provided the doctors approve*. With this I have to be happy but it feels like a small victory. Besides, a little voice deep down keeps saying, do I really want to go back to Bristol or do I just want to run away from Drake? What did he mean when he said I was too important to risk?

And anyway, if I run away what will happen to Chances? He needs me.

Emily isn't at school on Monday which makes being there a much nicer experience. There's no need to scan the corridors in between lessons, hide in the library at lunchtime or spend most of the day trying hard not to lose my temper and deck her.

After school I hop off the bus and make my way along the footpath which wiggles through the woods from Perranview Farm to the back of Chances' paddock. The bridle is in my bag and I've got the vague plan that I might take him for a hack. I'm still avoiding Drake who'll be schooling and Emily's safely out of the way too so nobody will notice what I'm up to.

"Chances!" I call, climbing the fence and dropping down into the paddock. "Chances!"

Usually there's a whinny and a blur of chestnut coat as the Arab hurtles towards me, greedy for the treats he knows I bring. Today though, the paddock is empty. That's weird. Where is he? Drake wouldn't be riding him and Emily certainly isn't. There's no reason to bring the horse in either. Unless…unless…

My stomach does a forward roll and I start to run.

"Where's Chances?" I gasp when I stumble into the yard. "Where is he?"

Drake's in the middle of talking to the vet but I couldn't care less about interrupting.

"Where's Chances?" I demand.

"Excuse me a minute, Dave?" Taking my elbow, Drake frog marches me into the tack room. "Where have you been? I've been calling you. Why haven't you answered?"

I ran my phone flat yelling at Alan yesterday and haven't bothered to charge it. What's the point? Mum isn't ringing any time soon.

"My battery died," I say and treat him to one of my best can't be bothered shrugs.

"Well if you'd bothered to charge it you'd know that Chances isn't here," Drake says, through clenched teeth. "He's been sent to the sales."

I can't believe what I'm hearing. "He can't have been."

"I'm afraid he can. The dealer collected him this morning. There's no way Michael was going to let Emily ride Chances again. She's only just out of hospital."

I couldn't give a hoot about Emily.

"Why didn't you stop them?"

"Oh come on, Amber! Grow up. Michael owns the horse and he's hardly able to stand the sight of it. What do you expect me to do? Buy it from him?"

"Yes! That's exactly what I'd expect."

Drake looks at me in disbelief. "You have to be kidding. Michael would have flipped and that would have been the end of my job."

"So that's all you care about? Your own skin?" I can hardly bear to look at him. What a traitor.

"Wow, you really do have a great opinion of me," Drake says bitterly. "No, not my own skin. I couldn't give a toss about my job but I do care about *my* horses. I have to think about keeping them going and where they're stabled. Six eventers aren't cheap to keep and Mike's my sponsor too. Without him, eventing's as good as over for me."

"Without us it's over for Chances," I choke. "You know what happens to unwarranted horses at markets."

Tears sting my eyes and I blink them back angrily. Think, Amber, think! "What market has he gone to?"

"Amber, I really don't think this is going to help. He's been sent without a reserve and he'll be sold," Drake says gently but I'm in no mood to stand around and listen.

"What market, Drake?"

"Hathleigh, but I don't think –"

I'm not hanging around to hear what Drake Owen has to say. Not when Chances is miles away, frightened and in terrible danger. Who knows what will happen if he falls into the wrong hands? Already labelled as dangerous he'll be either beaten until he fights back, hurts somebody and is shot or go from pillar to post until his spirit's broken. Both ideas make me want to be sick.

I turn on my heel and walk away from Drake as fast as I can. He calls and calls but I don't listen. There's nothing he can say I want to hear. All I can think about is getting back to the farm and finding Harry. Harry will know what to do and Harry will help me, I know he will.

He's the only one on my side.

CHAPTER 13

"This is a crazy idea," Harry grumbles. "I must be mad. Remind me why I listened to you again?"

"Because you know it makes sense," I say. "And we got have MacDonald's for breakfast."

"Now you know I'll do anything for an egg Macmuffin I'm in big trouble." Harry checks the rear view mirror and pulls into the middle lane of the motorway, the cattle trailer rattling behind his ancient truck. "And as for making sense? I hardly think so. I've busted you out of school, turned down a day's work fence posting and fed us both junk food. Your social worker will freak."

"Just tell him I forced you," I suggest.

Harry, who's six feet of muscle and broad shoulders looks at me askance.

"Yeah, right. Like he'd believe that."

"Alan will never know about this anyway," I continue, ripping open a bag of Haribo and fishing out some jelly rings for my driver. "We'll write a note and nobody at school will think any more of it. They'll all be relieved I'm not there anyway."

"I can't imagine why," Harry says darkly. "You're just so relaxing to be around. Hey! Don't nick all the fried eggs. I like those."

I pick several out and, blowing dust and hay seeds off the dashboard, line them up. Sacrificing the Haribo Starmix fried eggs is the least I can do since Harry's agreed to drive me to Hatherleigh Market for the horse sale. He didn't take much persuading either, especially when he discovered Drake Owen was the cause of all my problems.

"Calm down!" Harry said when I tore into his workshop, babbling. "I can't understand a word you're saying." Abandoning the piece of chain he'd been walloping with a sledge hammer, Harry placed his hand in the small of my back and guided me towards the bale of straw which he used as a makeshift seat. "Take a deep breath. What's happened?"

Somehow I'd managed to gabble my way through the story until I finally I talked myself to a standstill.

"So let me get this straight," Harry said. "You've been secretly riding Emily's star horse at night? And then you jumped it and she was so jealous she had to prove she was better than you to impress lover boy?"

I hadn't seen it quite this but his explanation made sense.

"Then she comes a cropper and *Drake*," Harry practically hissed the name, "sends the horse to market? How absolutely typical."

"That wasn't quite what happened. Michael sold Chances," I said. I was annoyed with Drake for not standing up for the Arab but it wasn't all his fault.

Harry's top lip curled. "Drake Owen could have stopped him. He's not to be trusted Amber. I did try and warn you."

I hung my head. "I'm sorry. I should have listened. It was just the horses were there and if you could only see what Chances is capable of. He's incredible."

"So are you if you can jump a lunatic horse like that without a saddle and without killing yourself. I've seen the horse you mean. It's the chestnut one Emily's terrified of, isn't it? Looks like its about to explode at any minute?"

"That's Chances," I said and a knot tightened in my throat. "He's amazing."

"When Dad was alive we used to have a couple of horses. He'd hunt sometimes and Mum rode too when she was younger. We sold them after...after the accident and we only kept Treacle because he's so ancient." Harry had a far away expression on his face. "He knew about horses and I bet Dad would have loved that Arab. He liked them a bit crazy. He'd have liked you too."

"Really?" I was taken aback. Not many people liked me. In fact, until a few days ago when he came home with Scally I would have said that Harry was one of them.

But Harry was looking serious. "Yes, really. Don't sound so surprised. You're not so bad once you stop trying to pick fights with everyone. You look a lot better now you've stopped channeling your inner Goth too. You're actually quite pretty when you're not scowling."

I wasn't sure whether to be pleased or insulted. Quite pretty? Scowling? Goth?

"You're doing it right now," he added. "Scowling, I mean, not being Morticia Addams. Hopefully we've seen the back of her."

"You'd be scowling too if your horse was off to the market," I said, ignoring that remark.

He raised an eyebrow. "Your horse?"

"He feels like mine." How could I explain that when I rode Chances it felt as though we were one? A beast from myth or legend, flying over gates like Pegasus and racing through the forest like outlaws from ancient times? Or how when he laid his head on my shoulder and let me brush his face, the gentle oat sweet breath and total trust made my heart swell? Chances might technically belong to Michael Lacey but in my soul I knew he belonged to me just as I belonged to him.

"So we need to rescue him." Harry strode across the workshop and picked up his phone. "Where's this market?"

I dabbed my eyes on my sleeve. "It's at Hathleigh and it's tomorrow."

"OK," said Harry. "That's only a few hours away. It's near Exeter and it's one of the smaller stock markets. I go there sometimes so Mum won't think it's odd. If we leave around school time we'll be there in time to grab a programme and find Chances."

I hardly dared believe he was saying this. "And then what?"

"Then we'll cross that bridge when we come to it," he said firmly. "OK?"

"OK," I nodded. I already felt brighter. At least we had a bit of a plan. The rest I would work out when we reached the market.

But now, as Harry pulls off the M5 and heads through the industrial wastelands of Hathleigh, I'm still trying to work out what to do. I've downloaded a programme and Chances is number fifteen, with no reserve price, not that this makes much difference to me. He could be twenty quid or twenty million quid. Either way I can't buy him. Short of leaping onto him in the sale ring and jumping out to gallop away, I'm a bit short on cunning plans.

"This is it," Harry says when we pull up outside a large grey building that looks more like an industrial unit than a cattle market. Only the lorries and trailers parked alongside give its purpose away. "Ready?"

Err, no. Not really.

"Absolutely," I fib, hopping out of the cab and clutching my print out of the sale programme.

We cross the car park, walk through an arch way before pushing open heavy glass doors. Instantly the smell of dung and urine and hot frightened horse hit my nose like a punch and a cacophony of excited voices and shouts fill my ears.

"Welcome to the glam world of cattle markets," Harry says. "Come on. We need to register."

"What for?"

"You really are new to this, aren't you?"

"You've been to the Shakespeare Estate. Not a lot of horse sales going on," I point out.

"Fair point," Harry agrees. "We have to register a bank card to get a number in case we want to buy anything. So don't twitch or waggle too much during the auctions, OK? If you do they'll think you're bidding. That is why we're here? I thought you came here to rescue Chances?"

Yes, this is the idea but quite how I'll do this is anyone's guess. While Harry registers us and has his bank card swiped, I chew the skin around my nails and observe the bustling market. Men in pork pie hats and tweed jackets pour over programs, iron shod hooves clatter across concrete as horses are trotted up and down and shrill whinnies echo from the barred stalls beyond. The air is thick with the scent of frying onions and burgers. There's a carnival atmosphere but it's tinged with an edge of despair too and there's a whiff of danger lurking beneath the veneer of respectability. This is not somewhere you want your horse to go; this is where horses with no other options and very little hope end up.

It reminds me a bit of the Shakespeare Estate.

"All done," says Harry, tucking his wallet into his back pocket. "Right. Let's see if we can find Chances. Number fifteen."

In his waxed jacket, country boots and tweed cap Harry totally fits in and as we walk through he's greeted by farmers and wiry looking jockey types. I'm doing my best not to look at all the horses and ponies standing in the pens and stalls. Their utter dejection breaks my heart. If I could buy them all, I would.

"Eleven to Twenty must be the next aisle," says Harry and sure enough as we turn the corner we hear the crash of hooves against bars as Chances lashes out in fury.

"Easy, boy! Easy!" I fly down the aisle and without thinking twice let myself into his pen, narrowly missing flying front legs when he rears up. His eyes are wild with terror, he's dripping with sweat from box walking and on his flanks are livid welts where someone's hit him. I'm filled with white hot fury. If I knew who'd got him into this state I could kill them with my bare hands.

"Shh, little boy. Steady little horse."

Harry slips in beside me and lays a gentle hand on Chances' flank. The horse shudders beneath his touch but quietens, sides still heaving and blood red nostrils flared in terror.

"Poor old boy," Harry says gently. "Poor old Chances. What a bad day you're having."

I can't speak because I'm so angry. How could Drake let this happen?

"Do you like the horse, Miss?" A lanky man with closely cropped brown hair leans on the gate and regards me with the beady black eyes of a crafty rat. "He's a nice animal. Would do anything, a horse like that. Pop a jump. Hack. Do a show. You won't go wrong with him. He's a bargain."

"This horse is unwarranted. What did it do? Kill someone?"

I haven't heard Harry speak like this before. He's quiet but there's an edge of steel beneath his words.

The man shrugs. "Nothing, mate. Probably just too spirited for the last owner. Arabs aren't to everyone's taste but he's a nice looking animal."

Two women join us at the gate, pointing out Chances' confirmation in strident voices.

"He's half wild. Seems to me he's barely broken." Harry sounds as though he couldn't be less interested in Chances. "Will you ride him in the ring and show him off?"

A shifty look crosses the man's sharp features. "He hasn't come with any tack."

"Not rideable, then. Good luck getting that one sold," says Harry loudly.

The two women exchange worried looks and turn away. A horse whinnies and Chances calls back, charging to the front of the stall and almost trampling me in the process. A lady dressed in Ariat and her teenaged daughter scuttle past hastily. The ratty man shoots Harry an ugly look and hurries after them, turning their attention to the listless bay mare across the aisle.

I'm confused. "What was all that about?" I thought you liked Chances?"

"That's Mick Ellory," Harry tells me. "He's a dealer and a really slippery character. If he so much as sees your eyelash twitch he'll double his price and you'll never get Chances back then. Come on, let's grab a coffee and find a seat in the ring."

By the time we sit down the auction room's really crowded. Tiers of seats are circled around a small sandy area where horses are ridden while the bidding takes place. Harry and I find seats in the third row and settle back to watch. It's all new to me and I have no idea what the auctioneer is saying because it sounds like gobbledygook. All the farmers, dealers and horse people seem to understand perfectly though and Harry translates for me.

"Mare twelve years old, by Floral Mafia, fifteen hands was BSJA," he whispers as a wild eyed bay canters around the ring. She's not sound but nobody seems too bothered. The garbled words increase in speed, there's a flurry of nodding and programme waving and then the gavel comes down with a bang.

"Sold for seven hundred quid," Harry says in disbelief. "Hopefully to somebody nice but you never know. The meat man's never far away here."

My stomach freefalls as though I'm bungee jumping without a chord. I have to save Chances. I have to.

More horses come and go. Some are ridden by a girl dressed in cream breeches and a black show jacket and those ones go for a lot more money. Others trot around listlessly, prodded by a stick, and a gangly foal steals the show by lying down.

"He's next," Harry says, pointing at the entry in the program.

He doesn't need to tell me. There's a flare of bright chestnut coat and the flash of iron hooves as Chances erupts into the ring. Rider less, he tears around, his legs smacking onto the boards and snorting wildly. Round and around he goes, so fast I'm dizzy just watching.

I clutch Harry's arm. "He's going to trip and break a leg!"

The bidding has started in a jumbled blur of sound. I see a nod across the ring and a wave of a programme. Is one of those bidders the meat man? How can I tell? It's not like he's turned up in a blood stained apron and is waving a cleaver. I have to do something!

I raise my programme and look straight at the auctioneer who inclines his head and babbles some more. There's nodding, waving, tapping and although I don't know what's going on I raise the programme again.

"You do know you've bid?" Harry says but I hardly hear him, all I can think about is rescuing Chances. As the speed of the bidding increases he seems to whirl around the ring in perfect time with the frantic words and I wave and wave and wave until there's a sudden thwack of the hammer against wood. Even a newbie like me can understand the word *sold*.

Oops.

"What's happening?" I whisper.

Harry looks at me. "What do you think? You've bought a horse."

I think my heart almost stops. "What?"

"You've bought Chances."

I thought that was what he said.

"How much have I spent?" I ask, and I sound like one of the Chipmunks.

"Two grand," says Harry.

Two grand? What have I done?

"Two grand? I don't have two grand."

Harry passes me our registration card and gives me a big smile. His blue eyes crinkle and the freckles on his nose jiggle and dance. Even his shaggy blonde hair looks happy.

"Lucky I do then and for that price Chances had better be as good as you say he is!"

CHAPTER 14

"I can't pay you back," I say to Harry as we squeeze along the row and make our way to the sales office. "I haven't got any money at all and now I've quit my job at the yard..."

I pause as a nasty thought occurs since from what I've seen the Crewes don't have any money either. "You're not putting this on a credit card, are you?"

Credit cards are something I do know about. The first time Mum was really ill she went wild with about three of them. I had no idea until I was delving under the sink for a cloth and a whole pile of unpaid bills fell out. Dogood spent months trying to unravel the mess and the weirdest thing was I couldn't even work out what Mum had been buying. The thought of Harry using one to help makes me feel sick.

But he just laughs. "You actually think they'd give me a credit card? No, don't look so worried. I've used my savings. I try to put a bit aside now and then just in case there's a miracle and something changes so I can to go to art college. I couldn't expect Mum to find the money."

I feel awful. "You've used your college fund to buy Chances? Harry, I can't let you do that."

"Too late! You've already bid," he says. "Besides, how likely is it really that I'll ever be able to go to art school? You've seen how it is at the farm. Mum needs me there to work. We'll lose our home otherwise."

I nod but I don't feel any better.

"Anyway," Harry adds, "let's look at it a bit differently. You tell me the horse is brilliant and that Drake thinks you're talented. My opinion of him as a human being aside, he knows what he's talking about when it comes to horses so this is an investment opportunity. If we get this right then Chances will soon be double what I'm about to pay."

We're in the line for the office now. There's no going back.

"He *is* good," I say, excitedly. "He's really good! You should see him jump, Harry! He's amazing. I've never ridden anything like him. And he's fast too."

"Well, there you go," says Harry. "It's my lucky day. You'll win everything, get loads of prize money and make our fortunes so stop looking so worried. This time next year you'll probably win Badminton."

I laugh because I know this is all just day dreaming but excitement starts to fizz in my tummy regardless. Chances *is* brilliant and I know that together we do have that special magic. If I school hard, practice like crazy and earn the entrance money then who knows? Suddenly anything is possible!

I fling my arms round Harry. "Thank you! Thank you! Thank you!" and he laughs.

"Careful, Amber! People might start to think you're actually all right deep down!"

"I can't have that. My social workers would be really disappointed," I say. "They love a challenge. Let's keep this our secret."

Harry pays and pockets the receipt and then we collect Chances. When he sees me, he whinnies and tears to the gate with bright eyes and pricked ears. I throw my arms around his neck hug him tightly, burying my face in his warm coat and drinking in delicious scent of warm horse.

"You're safe, boy," I whisper. "You're ours now and you're coming home."

It's late afternoon by the time we reach Perranview Farm. Harry parks the cattle trailer in the farm yard and together we lower the ramp. Then I duck inside to untie Chances and back him out carefully. He's travelled well and although he's a little hot from being in the trailer he's relaxed and seems happy. He's eaten half a net of the hay we brought with us and now he stands in the yard looking around with interest and sniffing the air with wide nostrils. Treacle shouts from the orchard and Chances spins around in a heart beat, burning the lead rope through my hands as he dives for freedom.

"What's going on?" Kate flies out of the kitchen door, hands covered in flour and still clutching a wooden spoon. When she sees Chances her mouth falls open.

"We've bought a horse, Mum," Harry explains. "isn't he lovely?"

"But that's Michael's horse!"

"It's a long story but he's not Michael's anymore. Chances belongs to us. Or maybe more accurately, he's Amber's horse." Harry smiles at me, his crinkly eyed smile that always makes me smile right back. "I think you should pop him in the orchard, Amber. He may as well get used to being bullied by Treacle."

"But isn't that the horse that hurt Emily?" Worry lines Kate's face.

"Didn't the horse throw her in a really vicious way?"

"That's rubbish!" I flare.

Harry lays a warning hand on my shoulder.

"I think a lot of that was Emily's fault, Mum. You know what she's like."

"She lost her temper and had a bad fall but it really wasn't Chances' fault," I chip in. "Michael sent Chances to the market without a warranty. Anyone could have bought him!"

Kate sighs. "I don't think Michael will be pleased very you've brought the horse right back to St Perran, Harry. Emily won't want to be reminded of any failure."

"Stuff Emily!" I'm sick of being bullied by her. This isn't about Emily Lacey and what she wants. "Kate, I can't let Chances be punished; not when he's only behaving badly because of what everyone else has done to him. He's frightened and angry, that's all. He's a fantastic horse and he has so much potential. I promise when he settles down you'll be amazed."

My foster mother gives me a long, hard look.

"Well, that does sound quite a familiar tale. I could never, ever turn away anyone who was in that position," she says slowly. Brushing flour from her hands, she steps forward and gives the Arab a pat. "I guess it's a case of saying, welcome to the family, Chances."

While Harry puts the trailer away, I turn Chances out into the orchard. It's a far cry from the beautifully manicured paddocks he's been used to at the Rectory but it has lots of lovely old gnarled apple trees for the horses to rub on and to give them shade in the summer. I watch him trot across the grass to say hello to Treacle and Minty who've meandered across to inspect the new arrival. There's a little squealing, some head-butting from the sheep and several laps of the orchard by all three, Chances dancing ahead while Treacle lumbers behind and Minty does her best to keep up, before they all settle down to graze. I watch them for a few minutes to make sure they're settled before returning to the house. I've got a lot of plans to make.

Kate and Harry are sitting already at the table with mugs of tea and biscuits. Kate's still frowning and Harry looks serious. They've obviously been discussing everything.

"Here's yours," says Kate, pushing a mug over to me when I take the seat opposite. "Now listen to me, both of you. I'm going to say this once and once only."

Harry and I exchange glances. It looks as though we're in the bad books.

"First of all Harry shouldn't have taken you out of school without permission," she begins. "Don't argue, Amber, or try to tell me it was all your idea. Harry's eighteen and supposedly an adult. He knows right from wrong."

"Ouch," says Harry but his mother ignores him; she's far too busy laying down the law.

"Your attendance has been a big issue in the past, Amber, and you've got your exams next year so this is non-negotiable. If you truant again or pull another stunt like this, Chances won't be staying at Perranview. I mean it! This is no example to set Maddy and both of you need to think a little bit more about her."

Blimey. I had no idea Kate could be so tough. To be honest I'd written her off as a bit of a drip.

"Harry, you've spent your college money on a horse and that's your choice," Kate continues, "and Amber, you've now got to pay for Chances and that won't come cheap. He'll need shoes, feed, hay, rugs, tack." She ticks these off on her fingers. "I don't know why you quit your job at the stables but you'd better get yourself there fast and put things right with Drake because you're going to need every penny."

"We don't need Drake Owen," grates Harry.

"Oh yes we do!" says Kate. "He's a trainer and Amber has an horse that needs training. She also needs the money to pay for it all – unless you're taking care of that too? And paying entries to events and vet's bills?"

There's no way I'm letting Harry pay for any of this. No way at all. He's done quite enough. I'll go and grovel to Drake if I have to and eat a massive slice of humble pie. Whatever it takes to keep Chances, I'll do it. I'll even smile sweetly at Emily and scrub her stables with a tooth brush if it keeps my horse safe.

"I'll go over after school tomorrow," I promise.

"You'll go now," says Kate.

There's a note in her voice that says there's going to be no arguing and, catching my eye, Harry gives me a nod.

"I know! How about I go right now?" I suggest brightly and Kate laughs.

Her laughter stops abruptly when there's a knock on the kitchen door and none other than Drake Owen appears. Instantly Harry's on his feet and the two guys bristle at one another.

"Sorry, I tried the front door but there wasn't any answer," Drake says apologetically as hovers on the threshold. "I heard voices so I followed them. I was looking for Amber."

"Well you've found her," snaps Harry. "Now what?"

Drake looks awkward. "May I come in?"

I can tell Harry wants nothing more than to grab Drake by the scruff of the neck and throw him off his land but Kate is nodding and already offering tea. While Drake pulls off his Hunters, Harry glowers at him. He's taller and broader than Drake, who is slighter yet wiry and lithe, and I think it's pretty brave of Drake to come here.

"I've had a call from Mick Ellery, the horse dealer who took Chances to

Hatherleigh. He told me the horse was sold to you, Harry. Is that true?"

Harry eyeballs him. "I can't see that's any of your business."

I see Drake fight to keep his temper. A muscle ticks in his cheek.

"It is when the horse is one I know. Is it true? Is Chances here?"

His dark eyes search mine and I have the swooping sensation you get just before leaping a giant fence.

"He's here," I say. "We bought him at the market."

"You don't give up easily, do you?"

I raise my chin. "No. Some people don't."

Drake rakes a hand through his dark hair. "Look, I messed up and I'm sorry. I should have had more balls - sorry Mrs. Crewe – more guts and stood up to Michael but I was worried too. He's a difficult horse, Amber. You could get hurt."

Kate gasps. "Are you saying Chances is dangerous?"

"No, of course not - if he's handled properly that is. Then he's a star in the making but if you get it wrong..." He pulls a rueful face. "Then yes, Kate, I do think he could hurt somebody. I guess that's why I'm here."

"You can't take him away now, Drake. Chances is mine," I say.

"I wouldn't dream of doing that. You're the only person I truly believe has what it takes to help him," Drake replies. "Look, I know it hardly makes up for letting you down before but I'm willing to come and train you. I'll give you all the help you need to get Chances going properly and safely."

"And how much is that going to cost?" snaps Harry. There's an expression on his face that I can't quite identify.

"Nothing. I'll train Amber in my spare time. I'd like her to have her job back too." His lips twitch. "She's a menace at times but there's far too much bucket scrubbing for me."

"Not man enough to do my chores?" I ask.

Drake laughs. "You've got me! But seriously, Amber. Will you accept my offer? Can you forgive me for letting you down and give me a chance to make up for it?"

"Of course she can," says Kate.

"Amber?" Drake says softly. "Will you let me make things up to you and Chances?"

We stare at each other. Everything else, from Harry's loathing of Drake to my hurt feelings, suddenly feel very far away. Besides, none of this matters compared to being able to keep Chances and do the best for my horse.

My horse. Oh wow.

I hold out my hand.

"Yes. Of course I will."

We shake hands on it and I know I should feel happy but I can feel

Harry's gaze burning into the back of my hoody. Any hotter and I'll be in flames.

I may have made it up with Drake, have my job back and a trainer on side to help but it's abundantly clear my foster brother's far from thrilled. And strangely this doesn't make me feel very happy at all.

CHAPTER 15

"My goodness! Look at you!" Dogood's watery blue eyes nearly pop out of her head. "I hardly recognize you, Amber! You look wonderful!"

Charming. I must have looked shocking before because I've had about four hours sleep and have bags under my eyes Lidl could use. I rode for an hour this morning, mucked out seven stables and cleaned a holiday cottage too. My hair's wild because I then walked home in the pouring rain and I'm still wearing jodhpurs because Alan was already waiting for me, tapping his watch and grumbling, when I reached the farm. Schooling and paying for Chances is taking every second that isn't spent on school work and sleeping.

And I love it.

"I always knew your hair would look beautiful if you let it grow and stopped dying it," my social worker continues. "And you've taken your piercings out too. You look really pretty."

I'd almost forgotten about my piercings. The earrings kept getting tangled in the strap of my jockey skull and the nose stud fell out one day when I was mucking out and I never saw it again. The tongue stud I got rid of too – it was really annoying, bashing against my teeth when I'm riding.

I open my mouth to give her a snide comment but something really weird happens: I can't think of one.

"Thanks," I say instead and Dogood nearly falls over with shock, which is even more satisfying than being rude.

"Amber's really busy with her horse riding," Alan tells her. He's parked his car (a Prius, surprise surprise) and has joined us in the hospital foyer. "She's got a horse."

"A horse?" Dogood echoes. "What's she going to do with a horse when she comes home?"

A knot tightens in the pit of my stomach because this is a complication I hadn't counted on. There's no way I can afford to keep a horse in Bristol.

"It's Harry's Crewe's horse," I snap. "Can we stop wasting time? Am I seeing Mum or not?"

My social workers exchange a glance and Dogood looks relieved to see me back to my usual stroppy self. She and Alan have finally managed to arrange for me to see Mum and since it's half term they can't make the usual protests about my school attendance suffering. Anyway, it's been over five weeks since I left and they're running out of excuses. I've spoken to Mum a couple of times and she sounds weary and a bit spaced out but that's effect of her medication. She said she missed me and I do miss her, of course I do, even if there's a nasty part of me that sometimes likes not having to worry about bills being paid or what she's up to when I'm at school.

"Of course you're seeing her," Dogood says. "I spoke to Sara's doctor yesterday and he said she was looking forward to it. Your mum's been having a good few days and she's making great progress."

I take this with a massive fistful of salt. Mum didn't sound so great to me and I know her better than anyone. I hope they haven't been meddling with her medicine again. I suppose I could ask but they'll only dismiss my concerns because I'm a teenager. Still, Dogood seems confident so I'm probably just being paranoid.

The type of hospital Mum is in isn't the kind you see on *Holby City* or *Casualty*. There don't tend to be lots of visitors with flowers and grapes and at times it's hard to tell the doctors from the patients. Alan tactfully says he'll meet us in an hour and leaves Dogood to sign me in. Then we're buzzed through a set of doors and shown into a day room where half-finished jigsaws languish on tables, spider plants tumble from dusty shelves and *This Morning* blares from the television.

"OK?" Dogood asks me once a nurse has gone to find Mum

I nod. I've been inside enough hospitals to know that this one's pretty nice. I wander to the window and look out. Maybe I've got used to the wide spaces and glittering sea in Cornwall because these terraces of grey houses seem very cramped and everything's so dull, as though the colours have been muted. The sky seems low too and hangs heavy with cloud. I feel really lost, which unnerves me because this was home.

Was home? *Is* home, I mean.

Dogood sits down at the jigsaw table and pretends to be interested in piecing together a picture of the Mona Lisa but I'm not fooled. She's actually observing me for some report or other.

Amber was very positive today and seems settled in her new placement she'll write, or something like that anyway. She was once daft enough to leave her folder out while she nipped to the loo which gave me time to have a good look at my file. It made *The Hunger Games* look like cheerful reading and *War and Peace* seem like a short story…

Mum's taking her time. The nurse went to fetch her ages ago.

I fish my phone out of my pocket and swipe through all the pictures of Chances. He's doing so well. I ride him every morning for an hour before school with a bleary eyed Drake hollering at me and until the clocks went back I was riding afterwards too. Drake's leant me a saddle and I've marked up a makeshift school in one of our stubble fields. Drake's also made me a few cross country jumps out of junk I've salvaged from the barns. I've been pretty inventive and if Chances ever comes across an old sideboard or chicken coop out competing then he'll be well prepared. I'd wanted Harry to help but he hasn't seemed that keen to get involved. Yesterday I asked him if he wanted to watch me jumping but he said he was too busy. I wasn't fooled; he was avoiding Drake. Since Chances has come to Perranview I've hardly seen him.

Chances has settled in beautifully. Life in the orchard with Minty and Treacle seems to suit him. He's so much calmer, although he has developed a bad habit of jumping out of the orchard and wandering into the kitchen in search of carrots. Last weekend, worried about the wintery weather coming, Maddy and I spent ages clearing out one of the pens in the barn for him but Chances shouted so loudly for Treacle and Minty that we've had to bring them in too. Scally is totally devoted to him and spends hours curled up in the straw too. I don't blame her. It's cosy place to be and I've taking to doing my homework there in the evenings. Writing essays and doing algebra isn't quite so bad when you're huddled under a stable rug and listening to the contented munching of horses pulling at hay nets. Kate's totally in love with Chances and she's always popping down to the orchard with a handful of carrots while Maddy likes to groom him because, unlike Treacle, Chances doesn't savage you if you come within ten paces wielding a body brush.

It's all working out really well. Chances still puts in huge bucks and I've lost count of the amount of times I've come off but everyday I see improvements and I know Drake does too. He's sparing with his praise but yesterday he said I was ready to come out competing which is the highest praise ever!

"I'm taking a couple of youngsters for experience and it'll do you good too," he'd said. "It's about time we saw what you two can do over a proper course."

I feel a fizz of excitement at this thought. It's only a local hunter trial but it will be the first time Chances and I have been tested. Emily's going too on her latest horse, a well schooled grey that doesn't put a hoof wrong and Drake's offered me a space in his lorry. I was going to turn it down because I'd rather share a lorry with the Noro Virus than Emily Lacey but Drake's promised she won't show up until we reach the event since she always travels in the Range Rover with Michael.

I'm so deep in thoughts about tomorrow that I almost leap into orbit when there's a touch on my shoulder. It's the nurse and she's alone.

"Sorry, love," she says. "I didn't mean to make you jump."

"Where's Mum?" I ask although I already know the answer. It isn't the first time this has happened. It's not even the second or the third. To be honest I've lost count.

Mum's changed her mind. She doesn't want to see me and although I know she doesn't mean to hurt me – she's ill after all – I'm so disappointed I can't speak.

The nurse glances nervously at Dogood. "I'm afraid Sara isn't having a very good day."

That's nurse code for saying Mum's in a bad way. It's no surprise to me because this happens a lot but I've been so looking forward to seeing her and for a few hideous seconds I struggle not to cry. I know life with her isn't always easy but she's my mum and I love her. I wanted to tell her all about Chances and show her my pictures. Mum used to ride when she was younger and I bet she'd love him. She once told me that her family had always ridden. For some reason she'd fallen out with them, something to do with them not liking Dad I think, but now and then she'll tell me snippets.

"Sara's been doing so well too," Dogood is shaking her head, sadly. "That's why we thought it would be nice for Amber to visit her. Maybe just ten minutes? She's come such a long way."

There's an awkward pause as the nurse does her best to think up an excuse that won't hurt me. Well, there isn't one and it's time for me to put her out of her misery.

"It's fine," I say dully. "I understand."

I don't of course, nobody really does, but I try to. I know it sounds callous but I sometimes wish Mum had a proper illness that made sense to everyone. Or something they could see? A broken leg maybe? That would mend easily too.

Dogood and I trail despondently out of the hospital.

"We'll come back, Amber. When she's feeling better. Maybe next weekend?"

"Yeah," I say but in my heart I'm thinking that I don't know if I can do this any more. It's like playing an endless game of snakes and ladders and I'm so tired.

"Can I go home now?" I ask.

My social worker puts a hand on my shoulder and squeezes it. "Your mum won't always be this poorly, Amber. I saw her yesterday and even if it doesn't seem like it, she really is much better. As soon as she's better of course you can come home. That's a promise. This isn't forever even if it feels that way."

For once I don't shake her hand away. In fact, I'm so shocked that I barely even register it. When I said *home*, it wasn't Bristol I was thinking of.

It was Perranview Farm.

What?

Since when did Perranview Farm feel like home?

CHAPTER 16

I've never felt so terrified in my life. My knees are knocking, my mouth's dry and I think I might pass out with nerves.

"Right, that's your girth nice and tight." Drake lowers the saddle flap and I slide my leg back. He cricks his neck and looks up at me. "Are you all right, Amber? You're a really funny colour."

"I'm fine," I say, or at least I think I do because it comes out as a bit of a squeak. The truth is I'm a mass of nerves and have been from the moment we arrived at the moorland farm where today's hunter trial is being held. I'd not been able to eat a thing for breakfast and when we walked the course I was glad of this because otherwise I'd have thrown it all up. It was all very well for Drake to point out each jump and say each one would be fine, he'd ridden around Badminton and Burghley, but to me each obstacle looked huge and alarmingly solid. There was a tiger trap that made my blood curdle, a hanging log I was pretty certain actually came from a giant redwood, and an enormous wooden chair that must have been borrowed from the BFG.

"There's nothing over three feet. Chances will make light work of the course," Drake's saying now. He smooths the Arab's neck and gives me a reassuring smile. "Just don't let him rush into the fences but at the same time don't interfere with him either. Set him up for each fence but then let him choose his stride and do his job."

My head is bursting with advice and whirling with thoughts. I know Chances can do it – the paddock fence is far bigger than anything out on the course – but what about me? I don't want to let him down.

I feel like I've landed on another planet and, unlike all the girls with long swishy blonde pony tails, Musto puffa jackets and Range Rover driving mummies, I am most definitely an alien. All the other competitors have been doing this since they were fetlock high to Shetland ponies and they don't seem at all fazed by it. Take Emily for instance who'd ridden the course in the past and didn't feel the need to walk it again. While Drake and I tramped through the mud and examined the jumps she stayed in the lorry glued to Snapchat and with her Dubarry boots as pristine as the day they came out of the box. I can't imagine what it must be like to have that amount of confidence.

"Don't confuse confidence with arrogance," Drake had said darkly when I commented. "The going changes every time you ride and there's a couple of new jumps too. Having nerves is a good thing, believe me. It gives a rider an edge and sharpens you. People make mistakes when they're over confident. I have terrible nerves every time I compete."

I'd found this very hard to believe. I'd spent hours on You Tube watching videos of Drake riding, trying to learn as much as I could from the way he executed a dressage test or rode a grand slam course, and I'd not detected any nerves. His face was set and his focus intent but he rode with utter confidence and determination. If I could ever be a fraction as good, I'd be thrilled.

But Drake was more than happy to shatter my illusions.

"Really. I'm vomiting for at least an hour before a class. Ask anyone – Fox-Pitt, Zara Tindall, Emily King – seriously! Anyone you like. They'll tell you the same. I'm famous for it."

I'd felt a lot better for this. My stomach might be spinning like Kate's washing machine but at least I knew now this was normal. I was also so preoccupied with the class I'd barely had time to think about yesterday's visit to the hospital. Alan had attempted to talk to me but the last thing I'd needed was his caring and quite frankly patronizing explanation of my mum's illness. I think out of the two of us I'm the undoubted expert in that area. No, I wasn't upset. Yes, of course I knew my mum still loved me. No, I didn't want to try again the next weekend. Yes, I did want to go straight back to Cornwall. In the end I'd bunged my ear buds in, stared out of the car window and ignored him for the rest of the journey.

Anyway. That was yesterday. Today I'm headed for the hunter trial's warm up area wearing an ancient rugby shirt of Harry's, a pair of long black boots Kate found on Gumtree as well as a jockey skull and back protector donated by Drake. I'm not sure where he found them because I'm most definitely not his size but he swears they're spares. I would have believed him except that I saw the packaging in the tack room bin…

He's spent a fortune and he's paid my entrance too. Why would he do that?

I'm just on the brink of asking him when we reach the warm up ring where smart riders in immaculate cross country colours are popping their horses over a big fallen log. Instantly Chances is on his toes, dancing sideways and snatching at the reins in pure excitement. There's no time to talk now; all my concentration is instantly focused on keeping my horse calm.

"Walk, trot and canter on each rein and then pop him over," Drake advises. "Nothing more. It's just to warm him up. Do your best to keep him calm."

That's easier said than done, I think as Chances leaps sideways and tanks down the long side of the warm up area. It takes two circuits before he starts to listen and even then he's throwing up his head and yanking at the reins. Several times I only narrowly escape breaking my nose and when he puts in an almighty buck I lose both my stirrups. Only the sheer determination that I'm not coming off before we've even set a hoof on the cross country course keeps me in the saddle.

Drake peers out between his fingers. "What are you doing? I said walk, trot and canter!"

"I'm trying!" I gasp, but it's like sitting on a grenade that's had the pin pulled. There's only one thing for it when Chances behaves like this – I need to get him thinking and that means jumping. As he surges into a bouncy canter I turn him towards the log and he soars over it, easily clearing the jump by several feet. When he lands I keep my leg on, close my fingers on the reins and ride him through the bucks that always come after the first few fences.

"That's enough for the warm up. We need you alive for the real thing," Drake deadpans when I eventually manage to bring Chances back to a walk. He reaches up and closes his fingers on the bit ring, as though wanting to hold onto us both. "It's time to ride down to the start anyway. Number twelve has just gone through."

I'm number fifteen. Instantly my mouth is drier than the sand school.

"It's supposed to be fun," he reminds me. "You look as though you're expecting to be shot."

I would reply except Chances is bouncing with excitement and I'm too busy soothing him to reply.

"Shh, boy. It's nearly our turn," I murmur but Chances isn't keen on waiting and paws the ground impatiently. Everyone is looking my way, partly because his antics are attracting a great deal of attention but mostly because I'm with Drake. In his cream beeches, black boots and crimson colours he draws all eyes and the pony girls and pony mummies seem to do an awful lot of hair swishing as they pass by. There's quite a lot of eyelash batting too although Drake's totally oblivious to all this. Every ounce of his attention is trained upon Chances and me.

"The first jump is easy but keep your leg on and be ready for the bucking," he's saying. "The second is just a simple spread and then after that there's a long hill so let him have a good burn up and get the fizz out his system. You'll need to collect him up pretty swiftly through for the third one and ride him straight to the cattle pen."

I'm trying to listen but to be honest I can't process any more information now. My stomach clenches with terror. Have I got time to throw up?

Number fourteen is waiting at the start. He's a really smart little black pony accessorized with hot pink saddle cloth, neon pink tendon boots to match his rider's hot pink cross country colours. Her hair's even threaded with pink ribbons just like the pony's beautifully plaited mane. Silver stars are scattered all over the bright fabric and they sparkle in the sunlight.

I feel very underdressed. Harry's old rugby shirt definitely doesn't sparkle and nothing matches.

"What am I doing here?" I wail.

"Stop worrying," Drake soothes. "All the smart kit in the world won't get that pony round. You mark my words. Just focus on Chances. He's the horse for the job. You'll see."

Number fourteen is waved through and heads to the first jump, ribbons streaming behind her as she sets off in a blur of pink. It all looks wonderful until the pony slams on the brakes at the eleventh hour and she sails over his head.

"Told you," says Drake. "That's an elimination. It's your turn, Amber. Good luck!"

I gather up my reins. This is it; there's no turning back now. Chances feels like he's about to explode at any second.

"Number fifteen?" A tweedy lady with a clip board ticks me off on a clipboard. "Ready to go? Good luck!"

Chances is jogging on the spot. The instant I shift my weight in the saddle he springs forward and races towards the first jump, a simple fallen log, locked on with pricked ears and a stride that eats the distance in seconds. We're over it before I hardly realise what's happening and we fly the spread too before galloping up the hill towards the third jump. I press my knees into the saddle and settle into the rhythm with a smile spreading across my face because this is incredible! Amazing! Breathtaking! Whatever was I worrying about? Chances and I were born to do this! Each jump draws my horse like a magnet and all I have to do is sit tight and release my fingers on the reins.

It's magical!

The next three jumps pass in a rush of cold air and flying hooves, then I have to use all my skill to steady Chances and collect him for the canter downhill. We pop a big brush fence and some tyres then dive through the owl hole into the dark woods.

"Steady, boy," I whisper, sitting back as we drop down a bank and squelch through mud before cantering towards the rustic fence at the far side. Drake's warned me about the soft going here and the take off is already deep from where previous horses have ploughed it up. Coming in fast is asking for trouble so I'll need to pick the right spot and approach it steadily. Half halting for all I'm worth, I manage to gather Chances up so that he springs over just like a rubber ball. The course then veers sharply to the right where there's a style followed by the enormous hanging log but Chances clears both obstacles easily and I pat his neck, my heart bursting with pride. This horse makes every jump a joy.

The course becomes flatter at this point with lots of long gallops punctuated by jumps. There's a hay feeder, a log house and a roll top and Chances clears them all with ease. He's settled into a rhythm, no longer fighting for his head but waiting for me to pick the next obstacle and locking on when I let him fly. The gathering of muscle beneath me, the energy and power trembling in that split second before the leap and the rush of air against my face feel like magic and nothing else matters. All my problems fade away as Chances and I fly fence after fence.

There can't be many jumps left. I think I counted thirty-four in total when I walked the course and it seemed like a lot at the time but now I'd love more because I could do this forever. There's a jump that looks like a wedge of cheese, the enormous chair and the quarry's coming up fast. We have to drop down, leap a ditch and then jump out again.

"Sit back when you jump in and slip the reins," Drake said when we paced it out. "But gather them up again as quickly as you can because you'll have to have him under you and listening for the ditch and then the big leap out. They'll be on you before you realise it so don't lose your focus. You can't afford to mess up any element. And don't back off either. Leg on all the way."

Recalling all this advice, I push Chances forwards and we plunge into the quarry. My stomach's still somewhere high in the air but there's no time to find it because the ditch is coming up fast and all that remains is the jump out into the next field and the final timed section.

It's a big leap out, three feet at least, and we need impulsion and power for a good jump. I shorten my reins, collect Chances and feel him sink onto his quarters. Up he springs, I press my weight into my heels to fold forward and go with him but something's wrong.

Very wrong.

I lurch sideways as my stirrup gives way. All my weight is out of the saddle and as Changes hauls himself through the quarry there's no way I can keep my balance and neither can I recover fast enough to grab his mane and readjust my position.

My hands flail and claw the air. Then I'm falling sideways, hooves flash just above my face, the world dips and I slam back onto the earth.

And then there's absolutely nothing.

CHAPTER 17

"The stirrup leather snapped?" Harry's incredulous. "How's that even possible? Was it second hand?"

My head's still pounding from the walloping it took when I fell at the quarry and Harry's raised voice isn't helping. With every outraged syllable my temples thud. The paramedics at the hunter trial said I was fine, and I'm sure they're right, but even so I'm feeling very wobbly. I'm on the sitting room sofa, huddled under a knitted blanket and two dogs, where Kate's ordered me to stay after Drake dropped Chances and I back at the farm..

"It's one of Drake's," I say.

"So he sent you out on that course with substandard tack?" Harry's fists are clenched. He looks like he's ready to erupt.

"It's a really nice saddle. It's one of Drake's event ones," I say.

"And the leather just happened to snap? Yeah, right."

I nod and my brain swivels inside my skull. Ouch.

"When I put my weight into it stirrup the stitching gave way. There was no way I could stay on."

"Of course there wasn't, love," Kate assures me. "From what Drake's told us, nobody would have stayed on in those circumstances. It's really bad luck. He said you had a really good chance of winning too."

"Never mind winning. Amber could have been killed." Harry's face is dark with fury. "A broken stirrup leather? I suppose we shouldn't be surprised. Faulty equipment that kills people is what the Owen's do best."

"Harry, it was an accident," Kate says softly but her son isn't mollified.

"You believe that if you like. I know the games his kind play," he snaps and stomps out of the room.

I let his angry words wash over me and close my eyes. There's no point looking to blame somebody because my fall is just bad luck. The stress on the leather was too much and when I put all my weight into my stirrups it snapped. There's nothing more sinister to it.

Still, rational explanations aside, this has to be the worst fall I've ever had. Somehow I managed to drag myself out of the mud, catch Chances and make it off the course but the world was rolling around like a fairground ride and everything felt a little bit odd. I was eliminated, of course, but even if I hadn't been there was no way I could have carried on. I could hardly stand up, let alone ride. The event was over. Or rather it was over for me because while the paramedics checked me out and Drake took care of Chances, Emily had flown around on her new horse and ended up winning.

"You either have it or you don't," she'd gloated when she'd ridden back to the lorry sporting a red rosette and brandishing a cup. "Why don't you just admit you're outclassed? Go back to the circus where you and that horse belong?"

"If Amber's stirrup hadn't broken she'd have won easily." Drake's voice was low but there was steel in it. "Her round was faster and more accurate."

But Emily just laughed. "Shame she couldn't stay on then. Face it, Amber. You're outclassed."

That comment still stings and I curl my hands into fists. I do feel like I've let Chances down. He was going so beautifully and jumping with such heart. I'd never felt so alive in my life. Well, until the point where I fell off and ruined it all, obviously. I bury my face in Scally's coat. I know Emily's a cow and usually I manage to ignore her but I'm shaken from my fall and her words are pricking at me like poisoned needles.

Outclassed.

What if she's right? What if I'm not good enough?

"How's Chances?" I ask Kate, who is putting logs on the fire and dangerously close to setting her hair alight as she leans in to stoke it up.

"He's fine, love. I gave him his dinner and a hay net and he's tucking in," she says. "He's none the worse for what happened."

"Unlike Amber." Harry's returned and is holding the stirrup leather. There's a grim expression on his face. "Look at this; the stitching under the buckle's been cut. Someone's sliced it with a blade, which wouldn't have been hard to do and wouldn't have looked obvious. No wonder it gave way when you put your weight into it."

Kate looks shocked. "Are you saying Amber's tack was sabotaged? Couldn't it just be lack of care or that the leathers are poorly made?"

I feel cold all over even though the wood burner is blazing.

"They're new and really good quality. Drake bought them but they were too short so he put them on my saddle. There's no way the stitching could have rotted," I say.

"Don't take my word for it. Look for yourselves." Harry passes the leather over. Sure enough the stitching has been neatly sliced and in such a way that any damage is concealed by the fold of leather.

Oh. That kind of damage doesn't happen by accident. Somebody deliberately cut my stirrup leather. Somebody planned for me to fall.

"Who'd do that? Surely nobody would want Amber to get hurt." Kate is pale.

Harry laughs bitterly. "They would if they thought she stood a good chance of beating them. Come on, Mum, don't be so naïve. Isn't it obvious? Emily Lacey did this."

His blue eyes meet mine. They are bright with anger and the reflection of the flames dance in the inky depth of his pupils.

Would Emily really do something this dangerous? Surely not? I glance at the leather again and there's no denying that the stitching has been snipped. The sliced threads are far too neat for this to be blamed on wear and tear. She was also alone in the lorry with access to my tack while Drake and I walked the course.

"Why would she do that?" I wonder.

"Because you're a huge threat to her," Harry says. "And I'm not just talking about the riding either."

And leaving me to try and figure out what he means by this, he drops the leather into my lap and walks out of the room with Saffy at his heels.

"There's no proof," Kate says quietly, "but I think Harry may well be right. I'm going to call Drake. He needs to get the the bottom of what's going on."

I'm horrified by this suggestion. If Drake thinks there's any danger or risk he'll pull me out of the next competition, I know he will. There's no way I can miss the next event. Held at one of the country's most important agricultural and equestrian colleges it's the last big hunter trial of the season and the prize money is five hundred pounds. I know the odds are stacked against my winning, and it's little more than a dream, but if by some miracle I was placed first I could pay back a chunk of Harry's college fund. I can't jeopardize being able to do that by alerting Drake to the fact that Emily's a psycho.

And let's be honest, if he hasn't figured this out by now then he never will.

The other issue, of course, is that I work at the Rectory Stables. That's what pays for keeping Chances and also is building up into a small fund to help Mum when she's discharged. I can't lose my job so I'm just going to have to be the Road Runner to Emily's Wil E Coyote.

I'd better learn to run flipping fast because she's probably already planning where to push the next boulder...

"I'll be really careful," I promise my foster mother. "I'll check all my tack each time I ride and I'll make sure I never leave it unguarded before a competition again. I'll even ask Harry to take me to any other events. Besides, like you say, there's no proof. What will Michael say if we go storming up accusing her? And what if we're wrong? That would be awful."

Kate bites her lip. "All right, Amber, we'll say nothing for now but if anything else happens, and I mean anything at all, then you're to let me know. I'm supposed to be looking after you, remember? Not putting you at risk."

I think about the Shakespeare Estate and I surprise us both by leaning forward and giving her a hug.

"I've never been safer," I say and I mean it too. Harry and Kate are looking out for me and that feels good. Really good.

If Emily did cut my stirrup leather or has any twinges of guilt she doesn't give herself away. In the following days she ignores me at the yard as always, demands Drake gives her extra lessons and continues to do her best to make my life a misery at school. I ride as soon as it's light and Drake continues to be up at crack of dawn in order to coach me and go running. We're concentrating on dressage now and, although he has zero patience with the precise movements, Chances has paces to die for and the most gorgeous floating trot. If I can bring this schooling discipline into my jumping then I know we'll be unbeatable. In jump offs Chances has the speed and ability to whip around and make tight turns that showcase his Arabian inheritance.

"Next season we'll look into some one day events," Drake promises, dropping me off at school the next Wednesday after my lesson over runs and I miss the school bus. "Maybe even some indoor show jumping and dressage over the winter too. That way when spring comes you'll competing against me before you know it."

He smiles at me as he says this, a slow smile which lights up the golden flecks in his eyes. Drake believes in me and this makes me feel as though I can do anything. Of course, it's highly unlikely I'll be here over the winter as Mum is bound to be better soon and she'll need me to take care of her, but who knows what could happen? I even have this little day dream where Mum comes to live in St Perran too and has the little cottage by the sea that she's always dreamed about. Maybe I could ask Alan about a council house swap?

Yeah right, Amber. As if anyone from here would want to swap to go and live on the Shakespeare Estate. Dream on.

Drake drives off waving and, with a sigh, I shoulder my ruck sack and join the river of gum chewing, phone twiddling teens flowing through the school gates. I'd give anything to bunk off and hide out with Chances for the day but a promise is a promise.

There's ten minutes until registration. That gives me enough time to nip to the bathroom and try to drag a comb through my hair. It was raining earlier and my curls have gone crazy and I've not had a chance to put any makeup on. I probably still smell of horse too, although take it from me this scent is way preferable to the sickly sweet celeb endorsed perfume the other girls douse themselves in.

In the bathroom there's no sign of Emily Scissor Hands, thank goodness, and I turn my attention to making myself look presentable. I tie my hair back with a scrunchie and am just rummaging in my bag for my mascara when I hear the unmistakable sound of crying coming from a cubicle. Somebody is in there with the door locked and doing her best to stifle their sobbing. I should know. I've done it enough times myself.

I rap my knuckles on the cubicle door. "Hello? Is everything OK?"

There's a loud sniff followed by a gulp. "I'm fine."

"Maddy? Is that you? It's me, Amber! Open the door."

The bolt scrapes and the door swings open to reveal a tear-stained Maddy. Her shirt sleeves are drenched and the contents of her bag strewn all over the floor.

"What happened?"

"My phone," Maddy gulps, in between sobs. "It's in the loo. It's gone."

I stare at her. "What do you mean, your phone's in the loo? Did you drop it?"

The minute I say this I know the answer. Don't be so thick, Amber. Of course she didn't drop it. Somebody has taken Maddy's phone and flushed it and I know exactly who. Somebody who's such a coward she won't pick on me or face me as an equal on the competition field but would rather bully an eleven-year-old and cut through stirrup leathers. My temper begins to simmer.

"Emily did this didn't she?"

Maddy nods. A tear trickles down her cheek and splashes onto the floor.

"She was saying horrible things about you so I told her to shut up and said something that made her really angry," she hiccups. "Then she was really mean about Mum. She called her...she called her..."

Whatever Emily said is too awful for Maddy to say and she cries even harder, her shoulders heaving. I'm filled with fury. I hate bullies so much.

"Then one of her friends shoved me in here and tipped all my things into the toilet," Maddy sobs. "My books are all wet and my phone's gone!"

I'm shaking with anger. For weeks I've put up with snide comments, having my bag hidden, my lunch *accidentally* knocked onto the floor, scrubbed buckets, swept stables – the list goes on and on. For Heaven's sake, I've even had my stirrup cut through which, although I can't prove it, I know was Emily's doing. I've kept quiet though because I haven't wanted to make trouble for Kate but all of a sudden I realise what a mistake this was because Emily's mistaken my silence for weakness. She thinks I'm frightened and that's given her the green light to continue.

I should have spoken up and I should have told Drake. I've been an idiot.

"Maddy, we need to tell someone about this," I say gently. "We should tell Kate."

But Maddy wails all the harder at this suggestion. "I can't tell Mum what Emily says about her, can I? Anyway Mum works for Michael. If I get Emily into trouble, Mum will lose her job and what if Michael throws us out? Then we'll be homeless."

I open my mouth then shut it again. I haven't a leg to stand on have I? This is exactly why I haven't been honest with Drake.

"What am I going to do about my phone?" Maddy asks, mopping her eyes with her soggy sleeve. "Mum can't afford a new one. What will I tell her?"

Maddy's phone is ancient but she treasures it. She's right too, Kate doesn't have the money to shell out on the latest gadgets. Every penny she earns goes towards looking after the animals and the people at Perranview Farm. There's always delicious food, the house is warm and the animals are contented. In six weeks I've yet to hear her complain about a bill or spot a lurking bailiff. Harry was right; she could make loads more running bed and breakfast than she gets paid by the social services for putting up with me.

My fingers close around my own iPhone. It was Mum's once and the result of a manic spree in town on a rare occasion we had some money but what do I really need a phone for? It's not like Mum wants to call me and I can certainly do without talking to Alan.

"Here, have mine," I say, handing it to her. "I'll buy you a new SIM card when Drake pays me at the weekend."

Maddy's blue eyes are circles of disbelief. "But it's your phone."

"And now it's yours. What do I need it for? Chances is useless at texting. It's my fault they were picking on you anyway." Then a thought occurs. "What did you say anyway that made Emily so cross?"

"I said she's jealous because Drake fancies you."

I start to laugh. "Oh Maddy! That's rubbish."

She gives me a pitying look. "No it isn't. He's mad about you. It's obvious. Why do you think Harry gets all funny?"

Because he hates Drake? Because he's grumpy?

"I think you've watched High School Musical far too many times," I scoff. As if Drake or Harry or anyone for that matter would fancy me, a skinny girl from Bristol with carroty hair and freckles! I'm just about to add something along these lines when the door swings open and in waltzes none other than Emily herself, armed with her makeup bag to paint on a bit more war paint before tutor time.

"Been swimming?" she says to Maddy. "Or are you always this wet?"

I can't help it. My temper, bubbling away for weeks, finally erupts. Springing forwards, I grab Emily by the school tie and slam her into the cubicle door.

"I think it's time we had a chat," I say at the exact moment a teacher sticks her head around the door on a pre-registration sweep. Instantly I realise I've played right into Emily's hands; the triumph in her eyes tells me all I need to know.

I've been totally and utterly set up.

CHAPTER 18

Of course I'm put out of school on a fixed term exclusion. Alan collects me, wearing his best expression of pained disappointment, and as we walk across the playground I see Emily smirking from the tutor room window. I bite my lip and look away. By losing my temper I've played right into her hands, haven't I? She didn't need to sabotage me; I've managed to do that all by myself.

In the past I've always felt jubilant when I'm excluded from school, five days at home to keep an eye on Mum being a good thing, but today I'm heavy-hearted. I'll lose my job at the stables, I know I will. There's no way Michael Lacey will have the girl who 'bullied' his precious daughter within an inch of the place.

I'm close to despair. How will I pay for Chances now? How can I support Mum and Scally?

"This placement doesn't seem to be working out as we'd hoped," Alan says to Kate when he delivers me back to Perranview Farm. "Amber clearly hasn't settled. It may be time to look at a different type of arrangement."

I look up. "What do you mean?"

"You're sixteen in a couple of months, we could place you in a hostel. Annie Dowood could keep a close eye on you until Sara comes home."

"In Bristol?" asks Kate.

"Yes, in Bristol. That's what Amber wanted all along," says Alan, helping himself to another homemade cookie. "We should have listened to you, Amber, but Annie thought coming here would be good for you. A chance to be looked after for once rather than having to be the carer. I couldn't stay here myself – my waistline wouldn't survive!"

As Alan pats his paunch and chortles, I feel my legs turn to water. Talk about be careful what you wish for. My social workers are sending me home but suddenly I know for certain that this is the last thing I want. I've no idea how it's happened but Perranview Farm feels like home now. I want to stay here with Chances and Kate and Harry and Maddy.

And Drake, I realise with a jolt.

Especially Drake.

"There's no need to make a decision yet, surely?" Kate says.

"She's just been excluded for bullying." Alan is wearing his serious expression. "I think there's every need. We took a risk and it hasn't paid off."

"I am here, people," I say. "And I don't want to leave."

"I'm afraid it's no longer your choice." Alan picks up his bag. I've never seen him look so stern and I feel quite alarmed. "I'll be in touch, Kate."

While Kate sees him to his car I slump at the table with Scally at my feet and Saffy's head resting on my knee. What an utter mess. I can't tell Kate the truth because Maddy's sworn me to secrecy and I can't tell Drake the truth about the stirrup because he'll be really torn. He needs the Laceys in order to keep on eventing. He can't risk his career for me.

Either way I'm stuffed.

"So what really happened?" Kate asks once Alan's gone. Hands on hips and eyes narrowed she has the look of someone who won't be messed with.

"Nothing. Emily wound me up."

"Oh come on, Amber! Don't give me that. She's been winding you up for weeks and we think she tried to hurt you too but that didn't seem to be enough to make you react before so what happened today?"

I want to tell Kate, I really do but I've promised Maddy. Whatever they've been saying about Kate must be really hurtful and she wants to protect her mum. I get that I do. On the other hand keeping quiet is protecting Emily who's the worst bully of the lot.

"I can't help you if you don't tell me the truth," Kate says.

I stare at the table. "There's nothing to say. I lost my temper because of the stirrup thing."

She shakes her head. "I don't believe you. There's something you're not telling me. Why can't you just be honest? Why can't you trust us?"

"Stop going on at me!" I jump up and send dogs flying. "I'm excluded and it's all my fault, OK! So just leave it, will you?"

I storm out of the kitchen and into the farm yard. It's drizzling and as I climb the orchard gate I'm reminded that Chances will need a heavy weight rug for the winter and a clip too, all things I'll need help with and all things I can't do without my job or Drake. It's a mess. The social workers will send me back to Bristol and who'll look after Chances then?

I run across the orchard, throw my arms around Chances' neck and bury my face in his mane. Shuddering with dread at the thought of losing him, I hope with all my heart that I can think of something soon.

Maddy doesn't spill the beans and neither do I but Kate's no fool and she knows something's up. I would tell Harry but he's preoccupied with farm work and the next morning when Drake arrives the serious expression on his face tells me Emily's got her story in first.

"Is it true?" he asks, leaning against the barn wall while watching me saddle Chances. "Did you hit Emily? Is that why you didn't show up for work last night?"

"If I had she wouldn't have been in a state to tell you all about it," I say grimly as I fasten the girth. "For God's sake, Drake. Of course I didn't hit her. Is that what you really think of me?"

"No, of course not, but that temper of yours can get the better of you at times."

I stretch Chances' leg forward to stop the tender skin of his elbow being pinched.

"And I also know Emily isn't always the most truthful person," he continues tactfully. "So what happened?"

I straighten up. "She was picking on Maddy, if you must know. Some of Emily's cronies flushed Maddy's books and mobile down the toilet and I lost my temper. I admit it. I saw red but what kind of person picks on an eleven-year old?"

"Are you sure it was Emily?"

I give him a scathing look.

"Sorry. Of course you're sure. That was a stupid thing to say."

"Losing my temper was a stupid thing for me to do because it's just what Emily wanted," I admit. "Maddy doesn't want Kate to know what's going on and I've promised to keep quiet. She thinks it will make things worse."

Drake looks horrified. "But that's the worst thing to do. That's how bullies get away with it. You have to tell the truth, Amber!"

How stupid does he think I am?

"*I* know that," I say. "And usually I'd have totally told someone what really happened except that it's all a lot more complicated, isn't it? Seeing as Kate and Harry both work for Michael. Whose side do you think they'd have to take? Maddy might be only eleven but she's not stupid. She knows they can't afford to lose their jobs. Any more that you can."

"So she's protecting her family by putting up with it."

"Yep. So how can I do anything else? If Kate and Harry think I'm guilty, if the school think I'm the problem, if my social workers take me back to Bristol then that's how it has to be. Kate and Harry already struggle quite enough to keep the farm without losing their jobs too."

"You really care about them, don't you?"

I suppose I must do. I have no idea how it's happened either. When I came to Cornwall all I cared about was getting away again but somehow the Crewe family and Chances and my life here have all taken a hold on my heart. I love my little attic bedroom with its drunken sloping floor and wonky ceiling. I love the animals and the way even Michael the pig seems pleased to see me when I bring his food. I love warming myself against the Aga. I even love the quiet and being miles from anywhere.

Leaving's going to hurt. A lot.

I don't answer and Drake trails after me as I lead Chances through the weed strewn yard and to the stubble field I use as a school. The lights of the farmhouse shine gold into the grey morning and it feels so homely that I can hardly bear to look.

"It's not fair," Drake says softly. "Not fair at all."

"No."

But then what is? Is it fair that Mum suffers from a horrible illness that sucks the life and colour from her world? Is it fair that Harry and Maddy's father died? Is if fair that they still blame Drake's family for what was really a tragic accident? Is if fair that Emily has all the lucky breaks?

Of course not. But I learned a long time ago that life's far from fair.

I pull down my stirrups and spring up onto Chances, winding my fingers into his flaming mane.

"Good boy," I whisper and one chestnut ear flickers backwards at the sound of my voice.

"We've still got so much work to do too," Drake continues. He rests a gloved hand on Chances' neck and looks up at me, brown eyes filled with worry. "There's the competition next week to think about."

"Do you really still want to train me? What about Michael? He won't like it."

Drake scowls. "I couldn't give a toss what Michael thinks. This is nothing to do with him."

"Won't he be angry? What about your job?"

"That's my concern. Of course I'll train you. I was also wondering if…"

A flush spreads across his cheeks.

"If?" I prompt.

He takes a deep breath. "I was wondering if you'd think about coming to the Hunt Ball with me."

Nervousness spangles from his eyes and I feel touched. Touched and a bit taken aback. Is gorgeous Drake Owen really asking me to be his date for the Hunt Ball? Me? Skinny, ginger nobody me? When he could pick anyone?

"Is that a joke?" I ask suspiciously.

He raises his eyes to the sky.

"You're as prickly and as difficult as your horse! No, it's not a joke. I thought it might be fun. It's just a party really but it's a good excuse to dress up and I'll be able to introduce you to quite a few people who may be able to help you. The horse world's a small place and if you want to event properly in the future then you're going to need support and connections. That's how this sport works."

Oh! He's thinking about networking. That makes sense. It's not a date then, Duh! Of course not. Drake's my trainer. Nothing more.

"Yeah, fine. If I'm still here," I agree.

"You'd better be," Drake says. "We've got a competition to win, haven't we? So I guess the question is – are you ready to win?"

CHAPTER 19

It's dark when I wake up to the sound of Maddy's voice telling me to get up.

"Come on, Amber! Get up! Mum's made porridge and fed Chances already!"

I groan and burrow underneath my duvet where it's warm and safe and there are no big cross country jumps waiting to get me. I must be crazy thinking I can do this. There will be really good riders there today, people who've been competing for years. One girl from a Bristol estate and her crazy Arab don't stand a chance.

But Maddy isn't taking no for an answer. She bounces on my bed and when Saffy and Scally join her I feel so seasick have no choice but to give in and face the day. Kate dollops porridge into a bowl and I do my best to eat a few mouthfuls but I'm so nervous I think I'm going to be sick. I walked the course the day before with Drake and my dreams were full of of looming jumps, deep drops and yawning ditches. At this moment I can't think of anything I want to do less than to ride cross country.

An hour later, Chances is loaded into the cattle trailer we're cruising down the high banked Cornish lanes as Harry drives us to the event. The sun's rising and it's a bright frosty morning with iced spider's webs lacing the hedges and the ridged plough sparkling.

"You couldn't ask for a better day," says Harry.

I don't reply because I can't speak. As we pull into the lorry park I realise that on comparison to this the last competition was nothing. Lorries and trailers are parked up for as far as the eye can see and the cross country course is already dotted with competitors walking the course and striding out the approaches to jumps. Hard faced horsey women in cream jods chat to men in tweed jackets and country boots, the place bristles with Jack Russells and Labradors and I don't think I've ever seen so many Land Rover Defenders in my life.

This is a serious event.

For obvious reasons Harry's towed me and he's been an absolute star because I've been worse than useless so far. I was all fingers and thumbs as I attempted to fasten Chances' travel boots and when he saw the tail bandage unravel for the umpteenth time, Harry gently took it from my hands and propelled me into the truck before taking care of it all himself.

"Go and sort out your entry. I'll take care of Chances," he orders once the cattle trailer's lined up neatly between two gleaming brand new Ivor Williams models. "Go on. Have a look round too if you like, chill out for a bit. It's all under control here."

I do as I'm told. I'm so wound up I'll start to tick soon and the last thing I need is Chances picking up on my nervousness. Harry's right; I need to chill out.

I sign in and collect my bib before wandering back across the lorry park. The event's in full swing. Glossy horses canter around the warm up arena and I pause to watch them for a moment, marvelling at the ease with which the riders hold such power at their fingertips. Hooves drum past, bits jingle, leather creaks and my heart beat accelerates. Soon Chances and I will be in there warming up too and then we'll be galloping out onto the course with all the jumps ahead of us. He'll fly them, I know he will. This is what we do.

I feel a tingle of excitement that's more powerful than any nerves. We can do this!

A grey horse has entered the arena and is cantering around in perfect rhythm, nose tucked into his chest and powerful hocks tracking up beneath him. His tack gleams, the five-point breast plate is lined with fluffy sheepskin and there's not so much as a speck of dirt on the brand new cross country boots that guard his unblemished legs. The rider is equally glossy in her midnight blue cross country colours and gleaming leather boots and as she puts the horse over the practice fence with ease her blonde pony tail streams behind her.

It's Emily, of course, and she's loving the fact that everyone is watching her. She certainly looks the part. She's been sweeping the board with this latest horse and I can see why. He might not have the fire and sparkle of Chances but he's schooled to within an inch of his life and with that Dutch gag on the bottom ring, he's going nowhere.

Whereas for me it's death by snaffle...

"Stop it." Drake has joined me at the side of the collecting ring.

"Stop what?"

"Comparing yourself to Emily and all the others. All the kit and money in the world can't compare to Chances' talent. Or yours. Believe in him, Amber, and believe in yourself."

I do believe in Chances. Believing in myself is not quite as easy.

"If I didn't think you could do this I wouldn't be here now rooting for you to win," Drake adds.

"You're rooting for me to win? What about Team Rectory? Do they know they have a traitor in their midst?"

"I think they have a few suspicions but I'm beyond caring what they think," Drake shrugs before he leans forward and brushes my cheek with his lips. "Good luck, Amber. And remember! Two jumps only. That's all Chances needs."

He turns away and heads back to Emily, who's pulled up shouting something about needing a breast girth. I stare after him in total surprise, my hand rising to my cheek where his mouth touched it only seconds earlier. Two months ago I was sneaking glimpses of articles about Drake Owen from the pages of equestrian magazines and now he's asking me to hunt balls and telling me he wants me to win and kissing me? I know it's just a peck on the cheek but even so! Things like this don't tend to happen to girls from the Shakespeare Estate.

Feeling like I'm walking on air I practically float across the showground and back to the lorry park where Harry has unloaded Chances and tacked him up.

"You look a lot more cheerful," he remarks, straightening up from fastening tendon boots.

I feel a lot more cheerful. The cross country course is still terrifying and the other competitors with their serious expressions and smart kit just as intimidating but none of this matters any more. Drake believes in me one hundred percent, just as my horse does, and I know I can do this. I can hardly wait to get going.

"I just want to get on with it."

Harry nods. "The hanging about is the worst bit, isn't it? It's like waiting to go in to the dentist. Come on, let's get you on board."

I zip up my body protector and pull my bib over the top. Then it's jockey skull on, medical arm band in place and that's it - I'm ready to go. Harry holds the stirrup for me as I mount and walks at Chances' shoulder through the crowds to the practice ring. Horses and people are milling around but there's no sign of Drake or Emily which means she must be on the course. At least this time I know she's not had a chance to go anywhere near my tack. I warm up and jump the practice fence twice but it's getting crowded and Chances starts to dance sideways and snatch at the reins so I follow Drake's advice and take the horse out again to calm down. While I soothe Chances, Harry watches the other competitors with a critical eye.

"Chances can jump better than anything in there. You'll be fine."

My stomach does a little flip. "The jumps on the course are huge."

"That won't faze him," Harry says firmly. "Or you. You're the bravest person I know."

"Me? I don't think so."

"No, I mean it. You are." He tilts his head and looks up at me, his laughing blue eyes serious. "I know we got off to a bad start and you were a total pain in the backside but I've always known you've been up against it."

"You read my file though," I say accusingly.

"Of course I did. Wouldn't you have done the same in my shoes?"

I can't deny it. "But all that stuff, those things..." my voice tails off as I struggle to put what I feel into words. "It's all true but I don't want to *just* be that person. I don't want people to look at me and feel pity. No way. I'd rather they all thought I was just a pain in the backside."

"Oh you're still that, don't worry. Look at the state of my college account if you don't believe me! Or the fact that I'm here on a Saturday instead of working. Or that Mum is worried sick you're having a hard time at school and won't tell her what's really going on. Or that—"

I pull a face. "You've made your point."

Harry shakes his head. "Not very well. What I'm really saying is that none of that defines you. When I think about you it's your bravery that comes to mind, not the other stuff."

Now it's my turn to stare. I'm stunned he might think of me at all, apart from what a pain I am, but that I'm brave?

"I'm hardly that," I say. "I felt like scratching from this whole competition earlier on."

"I don't mean all this." Harry sweeps a dismissive arm across the showground. "I mean how you've fought to care for your mum for so long and how you had to come here and leave her behind. It must have been bloody tough. New school. New people. Worrying about her. That's enough for anyone to deal with. You've jumped bigger and tougher hurdles in your own head than anything you'll see out there today."

"Number twenty-two?" A round tweedy woman clutching a clipboard to her bosom bustles over. "The Arab? You're next so get down to the start. Chop chop! You can talk to your boyfriend later!"

She moves on to round up the next competitor before I can put her straight. Luckily I don't think Harry's heard because he doesn't look too horrified.

"Good luck," he says. "Go and show Emily how it's done."

As I ride down to the start, Chances feeling as though he has springs rather than hooves, I think that if we make it back in one piece that will be enough for me. I'm competing against myself and my nerves just as much as I'm competing against her.

"You can do this," I whisper to Chances and as I say it I know right to my bones that it's true; he really can jump anything.

A car horn sounds and we canter through the start. Almost instantly a big fallen log rears up in front of us and Chances takes off perfectly, soaring over the jump as easily as though it's just a pole on the floor. All my nerves vanish in a heartbeat and I laugh out loud at just how daft I've been. Whatever was I worried about?

His mane flying in the breeze like flame and hooves skimming the grass, Chances surges forward and flies everything in his path. He locks on to each jump with total concentration, ears pricked with delight and every sinew coiled as he powers us up into the air and then onwards. Ditches, hay feeders, tyres and styles pass in a blur of adrenalin and joy and the cold air stings my cheeks and whips tears from my eyes as we gallop onwards. I hardly notice the quarry or the style and the water complex feels little more than splashing through a puddle. The flowing rhythm of galloping and jumping is so natural and it seems incredible that we're nearly all the way around and now the final jump, a solid wooden gate, is fast approaching. I've never know time go so fast. It feels like only seconds have passed since we flew out of the starting box.

"Nearly there, boy!" I say, hardly able to believe that the course is at an end. "Just one left.

The gate is looming. Six strides, five, four and then I can't count any more, all I can do is wind my fingers into Chances' mane and hurl myself up his neck as he launches us over the jump. The we've landed and are racing towards the finish, the spectators pressed against the ropes at either side of the course little more than a blur of faces and their clapping a mere ripple against the drumming of my horse's hooves. Somehow I manage to pull up and then I leap off Chances, flinging my arms around his neck and burying my face in his hot neck. Nothing else exists except my horse and my racing heart and nothing else matters except for thanking him for carrying us today. It's the biggest course I have ever ridden and Chances made every jump an absolute joy.

No matter what happens next with Mum, the hostel and school I know I'll remember this moment for the rest of my life. It will see me through a lot.

"Thank you, boy," I whisper. "Thank you."

Chances nudges the crook of my arm for a treat and, unable to resist, I manage to produce a fluff covered Polo from the depths of my jodhpur pocket. It's the least he deserves.

I run up my stirrups, loosen the girth and then we walk slowly back towards the lorry park, partly to cool Chances off and partly so I can collect myself because I am literally shaking with excitement.

"You've got the fastest time!"

Harry, a massive grin on his face, strides towards us. Flinging the cooler over Chances and taking his reins from me he adds, "You should have seen Emily Lacey's face. You've knocked almost two minutes off her time."

I'm not surprised we were fast. Chances gallops like the wind. It's as Drake says; if he goes well and listens then he's unbeatable but he just won't be bullied. Force him and you will have a fight on your hands you can never, ever win. I have no martingale, no gag and no flashy gadgets but I have a horse I trust and my confidence in Chances is unshakeable.

If only it was that easy with people.

With Chances cooling off in his rug, Harry and I walk him through the trailers and back towards the practice arena. We stop off for cups of scalding tea and order big oily cheese burgers, oozing ketchup and onions. My mouth waters as I suddenly realise I'm absolutely starving. I don't think anything has ever tasted as good.

"You've practically inhaled it!" Harry laughs, reaching forward and mopping ketchup from my chin with a paper napkin. "Here, have the rest of mine."

I'm so hungry that I accept. Then we sip our tea and let Chances graze while the final competitors ride the course. The sun is out and the leaves on the trees glow gold and crimson while the sky is bright blue. How lucky am I to have ridden my amazing horse around such a beautiful course? It's weird because winning no longer matters at all; Chances and I have got around safely and he's given me the ride of my life. I'm so proud of him. We've won something far more important than a competition today. We've proven we can do this.

While Harry chats to some young farmers I listen to the commentary crackle over the loud speakers and I gasp and groan with the rest of the crowd. There are falls and eliminations and at one point a bay horse gallops through the finish without his rider and an ambulance lumbers onto the course. There are only two competitors left and to finish now and as I stroke Chances and drink in the charged atmosphere, I spot Emily standing by the judges' box. Her face is grim as she waits for the results and she's saying something to Drake who shakes his head. She wants to win so desperately that I almost feel sorry for her. I have no idea who is leading or what's happening.

It really doesn't matter.

"The last rider's just through the water and coming up the the last jump," says Harry. "He's fast and clear but unless I'm very much mistaken he's not as fast as you. You're still in the lead."

I hadn't any idea that I was in the lead. No wonder Emily looks like someone's just shot her granny. The girl she hates, riding the horse she couldn't handle, have beaten her.

My stomach knots with unease. I'd better have my wits about me when I return to school next week.

The final horse and rider emerge from the woods. They pop the gate easily and then the rider gives his horse its head as they gallop for the finish. There's another crackle of static from the commentary box and Harry roars with delight.

"You've done it, Amber! You've only gone and won!"

Chances snorts and sidles at the shouting and I'm fully occupied for a few moments just keeping hold of my horse.

"We'll have to celebrate," Harry is saying excitedly. "Look, there's a hunt ball coming up and I was wondering if –"

But what Harry's wondering I don't discover because he's interrupted by the arrival of Drake who is hurtling towards us.

"I knew you'd do it!" He cries, throwing his arms around me and hugging me. "Didn't I tell you how talented you are? Now do you believe me? Do you?"

And do you know what? When Drake holds me close and spins me around, I do believe him. I think I would believe anything! I've done it! I've won!

"I can start to pay you back," I say excitedly to Harry once Drake releases me.

"Isn't she brilliant?" asks Drake. He holds out his hand to Harry. "Look, we're both very proud of Amber today. Don't you think it's time we buried the hatchet?"

But Harry's face is stony and the sparkle's gone from his eyes.

"I buried my father thanks to your family, so forgive me if the answer's no," he says bitterly as he pushes Chances' reins into my hands. "I'll see you back at the trailer, Amber. I'm ready to leave when you are."

Drake's hand drops and suddenly the sun doesn't seem quite as shiny or winning quite as thrilling. As Harry strides away I really want to follow him but they're calling for me now and I have to return to the practice ring to collect my cup and my prize.

I've done it. I've won.

So why, all of a sudden, does it feel as though I've lost?

CHAPTER 20

Harry doesn't speak much on the way back to Perranview Farm and after a few attempts at conversation are met with grunts or one syllable answers I give up. I know a good sulk when I see one, although I haven't a clue what his problem is.

OK. That's not entirely true. I know Drake's Harry's problem but I thought we'd agreed that Chances was our priority? And hadn't Harry said himself that if he was really highly principled then he wouldn't work for Michael who employed Drake? And Harry knows Drake comes over to teach me every morning, he's even said a few curt words to him, so what on earth is his issue now?

I'll try again.

"Aren't you pleased Chances won?"

"Mmmph," says Harry.

"And wasn't he brilliant over the course?"

"Yes. I've already said that. You did well. OK?"

He leans forward and turns the radio up and the cab is filled with the thud of the latest X Factor charity track. Well, that's told me. Looks like it's a 'no' from him them.

I lean back in my seat and study the big silver cup I've been nursing all the way back from the agricultural college. Inside it is an envelope which contains a cheque for five hundred pounds which is more money than I could have earned in months of mucking out at the stables. It's going to come in handy now I've lost my job, that's for sure and of course I'll pay Harry back too.

If he ever talks to me again, that is.

Back at the farm, I unload Chances while Harry deals with the trailer. Maddy and Kate come running into the yard to stuff the Arab with apples and carrots and then they help me brush him down and take off his travel boots. Maddy's prepared a stable with a bed so full of thick golden straw that I could practically fall asleep in it myself and there's a feed waiting as well as a fat hay net. Chances walks around a few times, checks to make sure that Treacle and Minty are next door and then turns his full attention to gobbling up his dinner.

I give him a pat and rest my head against his warm shoulder. I think I could stand here forever and breathe in the scent of warm, contented horse.

"Enjoy it, boy. You've earned it."

"He certainly has," Kate agrees, smiling at me from the barn door. Twilight's falling behind her and the light of the farmhouse kitchen spills across the yard, inviting and cosy. "And so have you. I've cooked us a celebration dinner."

"We're having roast beef and Yorkshire pudding! And potatoes and parsnips in honey!" Maddy chips in excitedly. "And there's a trifle too. We bought all the the food this morning for your celebration dinner."

Wow. A big roast dinner with a joint of beef is really pushing the boat out. Kate's a great cook but I know she does her best to eek things out and to use produce from the farm.

"That was taking a risk, buying the celebration food before I'd actually ridden wasn't it?"

"I never doubted for a minute you'd do it." Kate says staunchly. "And even if you hadn't won we'd still have had a celebration dinner because we're proud of you anyway, Amber. Very proud."

The barn goes a bit swimmy and I have to concentrate very hard on looking at the toes of my riding boots. When I look up again Kate's gone and I'm able to take a couple of big gulps of air and blink hard. I check Chances' rug, scratch his withers and tell him how much I love him and then I head inside. Hopefully Harry will be in a better mood once he's eaten something. I know how much he loves his grub and if anything will cheer him up then it's a big roast dinner.

I pull my boots off, push the door open and pad into the kitchen. Dinner smells delicious and my mouth is already watering. Nobody is in sight though, unless you count Scally and Saffy who are slumbering by the Aga, and I hear voices drifting from the living room. It's a room we hardly ever use since most of our time is spent outdoors or in the kitchen and I'm instantly curious. I can hear Kate and Harry and then a male voice I don't recognize. It's loud and brims with confidence and I pause by the door feeling unsure whether or not I should go in.

"Amber?" Kate calls. "Is that you?"

No wonder none of us ever gets away with anything. My foster mother must have ears on elastic. I give the door a push and am totally taken aback to find Michael Lacey sitting on the sofa, nursing a glass of brandy and looking as though he owns the place – which technically I suppose he does. Harry's standing with his back to the fire and has his arms crossed. A small frown creases his forehead.

What's going on? Am I in even more trouble? I rack my brain for something I could have said to set Emily off again but, apart from beating her earlier, I draw a total blank.

"Ah, here she is," says Michael in a deep plummy voice when I step into the room. "Today's winner."

He says *winner* like you'd say *earthworm* or *toenail clippings* or, and this is what I'd imagine he's really thinking, *council house oik who's been bullying my daughter*.

"Chances won, not me. You must have been mad sending him to the market." I can't help myself. The words just spill from my mouth.

"I agree," says Michael smoothly. "You're totally right, Amber. Selling Chances was a huge error of judgment and one I very much regret." He swirls his drink and stares into it thoughtfully. "Call it the over reaction of a protective father if you like."

Personally I'd call it Emily being spoiled and petty. A horse isn't a tennis racket; you can't play with it for a bit and put it down or blame it when you lose and swap it for a new one. I can't bear to think what might have happened if Harry hadn't bought Chances at Hatherleigh Market.

"I understand," says Kate. "Any parent would feel the same."

I look from my foster mother to Michael. I have no idea what's going on but something makes my stomach cartwheel.

Michael inclines his head. He has a thick mane of salt and pepper hair and his face is red from the fire and the drink. Chunky legs are clad in tight olive cords, his salmon shirt bulges over his belt and I can't help thinking that he really is a dead ringer for his namesake pig.

"That's very kind of you, Kate. I appreciate your graciousness in understanding that I wasn't acting rationally at the time."

I glance at Harry but it's still as though the shutters have come down.

"What's going on?" I ask.

There's a pause. Even the clock on the mantelpiece seems to stop ticking and hold its breath.

Michael puts his drink down.

"I think we may as well level with one another," he says. "We all know Harry bought that horse for a song. What did you pay? A grand? Two maybe? You picked up a bargain all right, but then you knew that, didn't you?"

Harry regards him thoughtfully. "I bought an unwarranted horse from a market. A horse you sold because it was dangerous. As I recall it was a horse you couldn't get shot of fast enough."

"I over reacted!" Michael splutters.

"Maybe," Harry agrees, "but even so I bought the horse on the open market. The way I see it, I took a massive gamble and so did Amber. From what you've said, and your *trainer* too, Chances could have broken her neck. He was sold as a dangerous horse."

At the mention of Drake, Michael's face darkens and he shoots me a very ugly look.

"Our *trainer's* judgment's been well and truly compromised. I hold Drake Owen totally responsible for the loss of a very valuable horse. Believe me, his future at the Rectory is certainly in question."

Harry should look pleased by this but he doesn't so much as turn a hair.

"What's Drake done?" I demand.

Apart from champion me, train me and totally defy his boss, of course.

"He's lost me a valuable horse. One that we can all see has the potential to go far with the right team and the right jockey. You did a good job today, my dear, but that was more down to luck than skill," Michael says.

What a patronizing git! And I thought social workers were bad. This guy makes Alan and Dogood look like amateurs.

"Amber rode beautifully today," Harry says firmly. I'm so relieved when he smiles at me that my legs go all wobbly. I hate it when we're not friends.

"That's not in question," Michael agrees.

"Good," says Harry. "So you'll understand that as far as I'm concerned, she's totally the right rider for Chances. The only rider. Drake Owen would say the same."

"I disagree, young man." Michael reaches into the pocket of his pristine Barbour, pulling out a cheque book and an expensive fountain pen which he uncaps with a flourish. "Now, I'm prepared to put my money where my mouth is. What did you pay? Two grand, wasn't it? I'll double that. In fact, as a goodwill gesture, I'll triple it. What do you say? Not a bad return on your investment, eh?"

Kate gasps. I think I probably do too. There's certainly a weird buzzing in my ears and the room is going a bit swimmy and odd.

"Six grand," Michael declares, just in case we're all too thick to do the maths. The fountain pen is poised and ready to write. "What do you say?"

"I say you must want Chances very much," says Harry.

I feel sick. Six thousand pounds is a fortune. More than enough to send Harry to college. He bought Chances as an investment and that's certainly paying off. This will be a no brainer for the Crewes.

"Emily wants him. She knows she can do well with the horse and she regrets selling him," Michael says. "I promised her I'd put this right. She's very upset to have lost the horse."

Upset? Hardly! The truth is more along the lines of Emily can't bear it that Drake's been teaching me and she certainly can't bear it that I've succeeded with a horse she couldn't get on with. She doesn't want Chances; she just wants to make sure I can't have him.

This is about getting at me. This is revenge.

The pen hovers. Harry still says nothing. Kate is pale and I can see how tightly she's holding Maddy's hand. Six grand will solve a lot of her problems straight away. Maybe she can even send back troublesome foster children and have some peace and quiet? I want to rip the cheque book out of Michael's meaty paw and throw it in the fire but this isn't my decision to make. Chances isn't my horse, is he? Not really. Chances belongs to Harry.

"Look, how about I make it seven grand?" Used to striking deals, Michael applies a little more financial temptation. "That'll cover any bills and also the work that's gone into the horse while you've had it. It's a generous offer and you know it makes sense."

"I guess I knew a sale was always coming at some point," Harry admits. "I've never wanted a horse of my own and even if I did then a fifteen hand Arabian wouldn't be my choice. You're right, Michael. It's time I sold him. Especially now we've all seen just how good he really is. Like you say, Chances just needs the right rider to take him forward."

"Harry, I –" Kate begins but her son hasn't finished speaking. Instead he's looking at me and my heart, which has been lurching horribly, starts to lift because his blue eyes are crinkling.

"As Chances' owner I'd like to sell him to a home where I know he'll be ridden well, treasured and not sent to market if he stops winning or the rider has a bad day," he continues slowly. "But I'm afraid that home won't be with you, Michael. Amber, Chances is yours for whatever you want to pay me. One pound or five hundred pound or a half pound cheeseburger, I really don't care. Some things are more important than money."

I've never seen anyone's eyes bulge quite as much as Michael's do at this moment. They literally look as though they're about to fall out of his head although to be fair though I think mine are probably doing the same.

"How about a Haribo fried egg?" I suggest and Harry laughs.

"Done! You know I'll do anything for those!"

"Are you insane?" Michael splutters.

"Probably," Harry nods. "Living with Amber has driven us all a bit demented."

"But that's seven thousand pounds I've just offered you! It's more money than your mother earns cleaning for me in a year!" Michael appeals to Kate now in his utter disbelief. "Tell the boy he's being ridiculous!"

"I'm afraid I can't do that because I don't think he is being ridiculous." Kate rises to her feet and although her voice is soft there's no mistaking she means every word. "Harry owns the horse so it's his decision to make and for what it's worth I agree with him one hundred percent. Amber has made Chances what he is today and he's her horse. Nobody else's."

Michael's mouth falls open. He's not used to the word 'no'.

Hmm. Now I can see where Emily gets it from.

"Now," Kate continues calmly, "we were about to have a celebration supper and I don't want it to spoil. So unless there's anything else you wanted to discuss?"

She means her job and Harry's freelance work and the tenancy of the farm, of course. Michael holds all these things in the palm of his hand and he knows it too. I'm horribly aware just how much Harry and his Mum have risked themselves for me and I don't know what to say. Why would they do that? I've given them nothing but trouble.

For a moment Michael Lacey looks as though he's ready to combust with rage. Then he exhales slowly and shakes his head.

"I think my business here is done. I just hope you don't live to regret your decision. I won't make this offer again."

"I'm sure we won't," Kate says. "And we appreciate the offer, don't we Harry? And we're very grateful too. It was exceedingly generous. You are a very generous man."

Michael, wrong footed by this praise, looks from Harry to Kate in confusion. Unlike me, he can't see she's crossing her fingers behind her back and the wind's well and truly taken out of his sails. Suddenly cast in the role of magnanimous landlord he has no choice but to nod and be polite. It's neat trick on Kate's part and I'm impressed.

While she shows Michael out, I turn to Harry.

"Why did you do that? You could have made your money back and more. You've lost seven thousand pounds!"

Harry grins. "It's worth seven grand to wind Michael up! In fact, I'd pay double!"

"But that's money you could have really done with," I say. "Why did you do it? Why did you save Chances?"

The grin slips from Harry's face and now his blue eyes no longer teasing and crinkling, but dark a serious intensity.

"Because it was worth every penny to make you happy," he says softly. "That's why, Amber. I didn't do it for Chances. I did it for you."

CHAPTER 21

To say I have a sinking feeling when I walk through the school gates on Monday is an understatement. Michael might have taken no for an answer but I'm one hundred percent sure sure Emily hasn't. She had a big party on Saturday night – we could hear the music from the farm – and she's probably spent the rest of the weekend plotting something nasty with her cronies. I've not a clue what it might be but I'm going to be on my guard and there's no way I'll play into her hands again by losing my temper like I did before. I'm just going to have to make sure I'm about twenty steps ahead.

"Can I find you at break time?" Maddy asks.

As always her small freckled face is pinched with worry and she's glancing around the playground trying to work out if she can reach her tutor base without being tripped up. It makes me wild. Why don't the teachers notice what's going on? If they weren't so busy telling people to tuck their shirts in and to put their ties on then they might actually be able to deal with the important stuff.

"Of course you can," I promise. "I've got double science in Lab 2 so how about I meet you in the canteen? We can eat our break together."

Maddy looks marginally more cheerful at this suggestion and we part company, her to make a run for it across the tarmac and me to dodge the rucksacks and spit in the corridors.

For once I make it through tutorial without falling asleep. Chances is having a day off which means I've been able to lie in until the luxurious time of half past six. I've not heard from Drake since Saturday and now I don't work at the Rectory or possess a mobile phone I'll just have to wait for him to get in touch but I really hope Michael hasn't carried out his threat to sack him as Emily's trainer. She looks her usual smug self, sitting in the back row with her friends and every now and again they all look my way and snigger so I think it's safe to assume it's all business as usual.

I sneak another glance across the classroom and Emily smiles sweetly as she draws her finger across her throat. Predictably, our tutor doesn't catch any of this but only sees me flipping Emily a V sign, which leads to a lecture and a negative comment on my report card. Two more of these and I lose my lunch time, which is actually a blessing is disguise. I mean, how much of a punishment is it to spend lunch time with a teacher bodyguard inside the warm exclusion room rather than skulking outside and avoiding the mean girls? If it wasn't for the fact that I know Maddy will be hoping I can spend lunch time with her, I'd be tempted to get myself into a bit more bother just in order to reserve my spot in detention.

Anyway, it's certainly hard work keeping my temper but I think I'm getting better at it. As the bell rings and six hundred students stampede to their lessons I actually feel quite proud of myself for being in school at all. I'm still in the wrong sets, everyone hates me and I can't see the point but my attendance is up and Kate's not getting any hassle. The hostel idea is still being mooted and after my re-admittance meeting Alan's made it plain that the last chance saloon is shut for business. I can put up with Emily knowing that I've got Chances to talk to when I get home.

And Drake to teach me. And the hunt ball to look forward to.

I still can't quite believe Harry's turned down all that money for Chances. It's the most generous and bonkers thing that anyone has ever done for me. I know how much he wants to go to art school and seven thousand pounds would have covered a huge chunk of his tuition and paid for somebody to help out on the farm while he was at college. To give all that up for me…

No. Try as I might I still can't get my head around it. To be honest I can't quite get my head around Harry either. His mood swings make me feel giddy. He's the kindest and the most generous person I know and I could chat away to him for hours but then he goes all quiet and odd like he did after the cross country and I may as well go and talk the the barn wall for all the sense I get out of him. I'm sure it's because he doesn't like me being friends with Drake but I had thought we'd managed to put that aside for the sake of my training and Chances? Seems as though I got that wrong.

Aren't boys complicated? Give me horses any time.

My Monday morning begins with double science. It's a well kept secret that Biology is my favourite subject and, like Dogood often reminds me with that pained and weary look on her face, there was a time when I wanted to be a vet. Obviously, that's not going to happen now because I had way too much time off school in Bristol and at Perran Community Academy they've dumped me in the bottom set where I spend my time colouring in pictures of cells and hoping nobody dissects the cowering supply teacher rather than actually studying. As usual I park myself in the farthest corner and focus my attention on drawing pictures of Chances in my exercise book. There's no point trying to do much else. I've written my essay for the science competition, all about the physiology and fitness of an event horse, but I can hardly see the point of handing it because everyone knows supply teachers don't do any marking. In fairness to the supply staff, most of my real teachers don't do any marking either – they're far too busy with crowd control.

So I keep my head down for a couple of hours while chaos reigns all around me. I sketch Chances jumping and grazing and then I pull out a copy of the dressage test Drake has given me to learn. It's simple enough and if I draw it out over and over again it helps me to memorize it. Maybe I'll get up really early tomorrow and ride it before school? Drake says there's a competition at the Duchy College in a few weeks so it could be a bit of fun. He also says there's indoor showjumping too. There's so much to look forward to!

At this point the bell shrills and there's a stampede for the door. The teacher does her best to slow it down but has no choice but to stand aside or be trampled. I put my essay on the desk on my way out but I don't hold out any hope.

"Oops!"

There's a thud as my school bag is shoved from my shoulder and tumbles onto the floor. My books, pens and lunch box spew onto the gum freckled carpet.

"Clumsy me," says Emily. "Didn't see you there. You blend in so well with the dirty floor."

I ignore her. Count to ten, Amber. Keep your cool. Just remember who won the cross country and who owns Chances. Don't let her get to you. Don't let her win.

"Here let me help." Emily bends down and starts scooping up my belongings and stuffing them back into my bag.

"It's fine." I snatch my rucksack back and she holds her hands up in mock surrender.

"Only trying to help, gyppo. You carry on crawling about on the floor. It suits you anyway."

Her cronies titter and I clench my fists. I know she's trying to provoke me. She's hoping I'll fly off the handle and wallop her so I'll be sent back to Bristol and Michael can make another offer for Chances. Well, no way. I'll crawl on my hands and knees all the way back to Perranview Farm if it means Chances is safe.

I meet Maddy in the canteen and we eat our break together. It's relatively safe here because there's generally a teacher on duty and by the time our third lesson begins I'm feeling less tense. It's only social education, you know the kind of lesson where teachers have to tell you about human rights and democracy, all pretty ironic really since schools aren't big on either, and while our tutor waffles on I'm planning to take another look at the dressage test.

Unfortunately, this is where my day goes pear shaped. Instead of our tutor, the Head of Year Eleven and the Deputy Head arrive. Both women have Very Serious Expressions on their faces and immediately a murmur of curiosity ripples through the room.

"Good morning 11x," says the Deputy Head. "I'm not going to keep you in suspense as to why I'm here rather than Mr. Lewis. I'm very sad to say that a serious allegation has been made."

There's another half excited half nervous ripple. I stifle a yawn. What now? Bomb making? A shot gun? Or maybe even some sexting? Luckily for me I don't think they've banned dressage tests yet.

"Miss Dean and I are here to conduct a bag search," continues the Deputy Head. She scans our faces like Robocop just in case there's any trace of guilt lurking. "You all know how this goes. We'll work through in register order."

One by one students traipse to the front of the classroom where the teachers systematically empty their school bags. A couple of mobile phones are found to be switched on and Jonny Casper has a rotting lunch box but apart from that it's all rather dull. By the time it's E for Evans most students have lost interest and are chatting to one another or texting under the desks but as I make my way to the front Emily Lacey is watching me closely with a triumphant smile on her face.

Instantly my skin prickles and I see again my belongings tipped all over the corridor with Emily most uncharacteristically attempting to replace them. It seemed weird at the time but now it makes perfect sense.

She's set me up. What's she planted on me?

There's a sharp intake of breath from my Head of Year. Glancing down I see she's fished out a small plastic zip lock bag containing what looks like half a crumbled Oxo cube.

I'm not an idiot. I know exactly what this is. In my mind's eye I see Emily drawing her finger across her throat in registration and I think I'm going to throw up.

I'm from a sink estate in Bristol. I'm in long term foster care. Nobody's going to believe this is nothing to do with me. Who would anyone believe? Emily Lacey with her big innocent eyes and rich daddy or the scruffy new kid with a bad attitude and a mad mum?

Feeling as though I'm zooming downwards in a very fast lift, I follow the teachers out of the room and to the Year Head's office. Everything that happens next feels as though I'm watching it from a distance. Kate's called, Alan arrives, there's a Special Police Officer and at some point during all this I'm excluded too. While everything goes on I don't say a word.

What would be the point? Even Alan can hardly look at me and he's paid to be on my side. If I tell them the truth they'll just think it's another example of my bullying Emily. What can I possibly do when they've already made up their minds I'm guilty?

"This isn't working," Alan says once we're inside the Prius. "I don't know what to say, Amber. We've tried and tried with you but drugs?" He shakes his head wearily. "It might just seem like a little bit of grass to you but bringing that into school is a serious offence. Were you going to sell it?"

The only grass I care about is green and feeds horses. I've never touched drugs in my life and I never will. You don't live somewhere like the Shakespeare Estate and not realise what bad news drugs are. It's all so unfair. I've helped Mum with her controlled medication for years and I hardly even touch a Nurofen when I have a headache yet instantly everyone's happy to believe I'm selling drugs?

What's the point of arguing? Alan's already made up his mind and when I fail to reply he sighs even more heavily.

"Do you realise how serious this is? We're looking a permanent exclusion, Amber, and maybe even a police prosecution. It's not a joke."

Does he see me laughing?

"So you think I did it?" I say in disbelief.

"Did you?"

I laugh bitterly. "If you need to ask me then what's the point of saying anything at all?"

"The point is that this is your future. Your GCSES are coming up and we'll need to get you into a pupil referral unit really fast. I'll call Annie Dowood and see if she can get on the case. She can arrange a temporary hostel placement too. You're almost sixteen. I'm sure we can work something out."

"But Dogood's in Bristol!" I cry. Cold dread washes over me. What about Chances? What about Kate and Harry? Maddy at school alone? Saffy wondering where I am? "She works in Bristol."

"Yes she does," says Alan and there's a firmness in his voice totally at odds with the silly beard and hippy smock. "And Bristol's where you're going. You win, Amber and you finally get your own way, so well done. We're going to send you home. You're going back to Bristol."

CHAPTER 22

"I didn't do it!"

As soon as Alan drives away I turn to Kate in utter despair.

"You do believe me, don't you? I'd never, ever touch drugs. I didn't do it!"

Kate's answer is to pull me into her arms and hug me tightly. That hug says better than any words that she believes me. For a moment I almost break with relief because it's blatantly clear neither Alan nor my teachers do. As far as they're concerned it's a case of the problem kid from the rough estate reverting to type and the sooner they send me back where I belong the better it will be for everyone.

But not for me! And not for Chances!

"Emily must have done it," I mumble into Kate's shoulder. "She knocked my bag off my shoulder earlier and my things went everywhere. I bet that's when she slipped the package in."

Kate's usually smiley face is deadly serious.

"You think Emily knocked your bag off your shoulder deliberately?"

Wow, it must be nice to inhabit that parallel universe where people don't mean to be nasty. The look on my face must say it all because Kate then sighs heavily and shakes her head.

"That stirrup snapping really wasn't an accident, was it? Be honest with me, Amber! This has been going on for a while, hasn't it?"

"Yes," I admit. Like from second Emily first clapped eyes on me? She's hated me from the moment she saw me talking to her horses and when Drake was nice it made things a million times worse. She can't bear it that he's my friend or that he thinks I've got talent. That's what this is really all about.

"I think it's time you told me what's really been going on," Kate says. She propels me across the kitchen to sit down at the table. "And this time I want the truth, Amber. You never hit Emily, either did you? You were sticking up for yourself after weeks of being picked on."

I nod. Technically I was sticking up for Maddy too, of course, but I'm very aware I've been unwisely sworn to secrecy. What a mess. Now everyone thinks I'm a bully and a drug pusher and I bet Alan's on his hands free right now ordering Dogood to come and get me.

I can't help it. A tear trickles down my cheek and splashes onto the table. What bad fairy did my parents forget to invite to my christening?

Kate doesn't fuss or smother me. Instead she makes a mug of strong tea and places a box of tissues on the table so that I can mop my eyes and blow my nose. I can't crack now. I have to keep it together.

"I don't know why you're protecting Emily but it's time to stop all that." Kate sits opposite, places her mug on the table with a slosh of tea and pins me with a stern look. "I want the truth now, Amber. You know why."

I do. This is as serious as it gets. It's no longer about tripping me up, name calling or even sabotaging my tack. It's gone way beyond that because Emily's landed me in trouble with the law and ruined my foster placement too. My exams, already not looking great, are hanging in the balance and I could even end up with a criminal record. Alan's explained all this to me in grim detail and I feel quite sick. Can you imagine who a court would believe if it came down to deciding between me and Emily?

I can almost hear the prison door clanging shut.

"They'll never let me look after Mum now," I whisper. "I've really let her down."

Kate reaches across the table and squeezes my hand.

"Sara's got the help she needs right now. Let's think about you for once, OK? Now tell me what's really been going on, Amber. The truth please."

"OK," I say. I'll just tell her about what's happened with me. I'll keep Maddy's secret for now.

"And don't even think about leaving bits out," she adds.

"Are you psychic or something?"

Kate laughs. "No, but I've been a foster mum for a while now and you don't last this long without learning a few things about young people. If I'm going to be able to help you then I need to know everything."

And this is when something weird happens. Usually when I'm asked to tell somebody what's happening in my life, Dogood or Alan for instance or all the busybodies at a meeting, I clamp my mouth shut and say nothing. Now, and most unusually, the words are like a torrent and I find myself telling Kate absolutely everything. I don't edit events either. Even when I see how upset she is when I tell her all about what's been going on with Maddy, I don't hold back. Finally I talk myself to a standstill and when I take a sip my tea it's stone cold.

"I'm sorry I didn't tell you about Maddy before," I say finally. "I really wanted to but she made me promise because she's so worried Michael will be angry and you'll lose your job. I know I should have said something. It was stupid of me to keep it a secret."

Kate says nothing but there's an expression on her face that reminds me of Harry when he's really angry.

"I did my best to look out for her," I add. "I promise. I just wish I'd done more."

"None of this is your fault, Amber." Kate's voice is quiet but it's throbbing with anger and there's a glitter in her blue eyes I've not seen before. "There's only one person who's responsible here and I couldn't care less who her father is or what he might threaten. She has to be held accountable and I promise you she will be."

When I first arrived at Perranview Farm I'd thought Kate was a push over because she was quiet and kind. Now I know these qualities are strengths and that underneath the gentle façade she's one of the bravest and strongest people I've ever met. She's dealt with the loss of her husband, held her family together and kept the farm going. Kate Crewe is made of steel.

"But what's going to happen?" My heart's still racing with fear. "What about Chances? What about Mum? Where am I going?"

Kate picks up her phone. "You're going nowhere, Amber, except out to check on Chances."

"But who are you calling?" I can't disguise the note of panic in my voice. Has she decided I'm too much of a liability?

"Harry of course," says Kate. "The farm can wait because we need him here. Then I'm calling the school and after that I'm calling Michael. It's high time he heard a few home truths. This time we're not holding back and being polite." She raises her chin and looks me in the eye. "We've all been bullied far too long. This stops today."

I know better than to even try to argue. Besides, Kate's right. We've all been bullied one way or another and trying to pretend otherwise has only made it worse. Leaving Kate to make her calls, I wander over to the orchard where Chances, Treacle and Minty are cropping the grass, blissfully unware of the unfolding drama. I sit on the fence and watch them for a while and I love them all so much that even thinking about leaving them feels like a punch in my chest.

"Chances!" I call softly and my horse looks up, dark eyes shining and ears pricking forwards when he sees me. A visit from me always means apples or crusts of bread and with a whinny he comes cantering over, tail held high and mane flowing in the cold wind.

I dig a horse treat out of my pocket and fling my arms around his neck, burying my face in his unclipped coat and wishing with all my heart that I could just leap onto his warm back and gallop far away. That's what happens in fairy tales and pony books but we all know real life isn't like that. Where will I keep my beautiful, magical horse if I'm living in a hostel? And how will I be able to pay for him when I fail all my GCSEs and can't get a job?

I choke out all my fears and the Arab's ears flicker back and forth at the sound of my voice. Chances knows everything; he knows about Mum's illness, Emily's bullying and even how confused I am about Drake, who probably now believes the very worst of me and certainly won't be taking me to a hunt ball. And then there's Harry who's given up his college fund for me and been the best friend I've ever had.

I'm going to miss Harry so much.

I'm going to miss everyone.

And this is when my tears finally fall thick and fast, soaking into Chances' warm, chestnut neck. Only my horse sees me cry but I know he'll never tell a soul. He's the best keeper of secrets in the whole world and I love him so much it hurts.

It's an hour or so later before my face looks less frog like and I finally manage to stop crying. Chances has long since returned to the serious business of grazing and, feeling wrung out and wobbly, I make my way back to the farm. Harry's truck is outside the back door and beside it a very shiny Range Rover whose number plate bears the legend MIK 3K and which is parked at a wonky angle, suggesting the driver has screeched up and leapt straight out.

My mouth feels like Perran Beach. Kate must have called Michael straight away and told him everything. I can hear voices and the closer I step to the kitchen door the louder they become. I daren't go inside because this sounds like a full scale row.

And it's a row about me.

I've caused this.

"You don't know what you've started," Michael shouts. "How dare you accuse my daughter of bullying when it's bloody obvious who the trouble maker is! I've just about had enough of you filling my property with your waifs and strays and lowering the tone of this village. I've put up with it until now but harbouring a drug addict is one step too far."

"Amber's not a drug addict!" Kate yells back.

"She was found with a bag of drugs! You told me so yourself!"

"Emily planted that bag." This is Harry and although his voice is low it's filled with anger. "Just like she cut the stitching on the stirrup and then set Amber up as a bully. Your precious Emily's been playing everyone. You most of all!"

"Total and utter fantasy. Where's your evidence?"

"I don't need evidence. I believe Amber," says Harry and I feel warm all over.

Michael snorts. "A girl like that will lie through her teeth. I'm sick and tired of sob stories and excuses, Kate. Why's she here anyway? Parents in prison? Drug addict mother?"

I clench my fists.

"Amber's mother is in hospital which means she hasn't anyone else to look after her," Kate says quietly. "Amber's usually her mother's carer, Michael. She's not had it easy and little compassion wouldn't go amiss."

"In my opinion charity begins at home," he snaps. "Look, Kate, I know you mean well but this bleeding heart nonsense has simply got to stop. None us in St Perran have any idea who you're bringing into our community and exposing our children to and it simply isn't on. My daughter could have had drugs pushed on her by this girl."

"That's total crap!" Harry explodes. "It's far more likely to be the other way around! When was the last time you bothered to check what Emily's up to when you're away on business or who she invites to her parties? Before you start making accusations maybe you should look a bit closer to home?"

"Are you accusing my daughter of using drugs?" splutters Michael.

"I'm telling you that she's not as innocent as you think she is! She's a bully and a liar and if you can't see it, then you're an idiot," Harry shoots back and I hear Kate gasp.

Then there's an abrupt silence.

"Well, you've both made your feelings about me and my daughter very plain," Michael says finally and his voice is tight with anger. "At least we all know where we stand. Don't bother turning up to work for me again, Harry, because you won't be needed and Kate? When the lease on this place is up don't expect to have it renewed."

I can't bear to hear any more of this. What have I done? Because of me the Crewe family are going to lose everything that they love. I can't let that happen, not after everything they've tried to do for me.

There's only one thing I can do now; I have to get right away and hope that things will calm down if I'm not here. Kate will make it up with Michael and everyone can go on believing that Emily's innocent and it was me all along who caused all the trouble. They can think the worst of me and I can handle that if it means the people I love are safe.

Hold on. Do I love the Crewe family?

There's a real ache in my chest when I think about never seeing them again and I know I can't bear for them to be punished because of me so I guess that means I must do. You'd think I'd have learned my lesson by now, wouldn't you? The people I love always end up suffering. I'm like some kind of curse. Maybe this is why Dad left? Perhaps he knew that, like Mum, I'm bad news?

I bite my lip hard. If I still had earrings I'd be digging one into my hand right now because I'm very close to falling apart and that's a luxury I can't afford. No, I think it's best for everyone if I just disappear and to do that I need to keep thinking clearly. This is not the time to have a melt down even if keeping it together is the most difficult thing I'll ever have to do.

And if the mere thought of leaving hurts this much, then I'm already afraid of just how painful it's going to be.

CHAPTER 23

I haven't a clue where I'm going. All I know is I have to get away because it's too painful to stay for a second longer. Once Harry and Kate leave the kitchen I fly to my room and stuff as many of my belongings as I can into my ruck sack before calling Scally and heading into the orchard.

It's early afternoon but the winter sun's already doing parkour on the tree tops. My breath hangs in the air and purple shadows are starting to stretch across the grass. In just a couple of hours it'll be time to catch the horses and bring them in for the night, swapping their light weight sheets for stable blankets and tying up fat hay nets. It's probably my favourite time of the day and knowing that I'm not going to be here this evening to make Chances his feed and hear him whicker with excitement when he sees me carrying it into the barn, almost breaks my resolve.

But I know I have to go. Look how much damage I've caused already. If I'm out of the way things stand some kind of a chance of returning to normal

Chances and Treacle are already waiting at the gate. I let my bag slip from my shoulder and climb onto the fence, reaching over to scratch their necks. Greedy Treacle nips my sleeve and I cuff him away but Chances rests his head on my shoulder and I close my eyes for a moment, drinking in his grass sweet breath and the warmth of his glossy coat against my cheek. If only I could bottle this moment and save it for the rest of my life, something to look at and dream about in the days and years ahead. I know I'll never forget how it felt to touch Chances into a canter, releasing my fingers on the reins and feeling him soar upwards and over every jump. Whenever I close my eyes I'll see him floating across the paddock or plunging and dancing like a horse from legend, neck crested and hooves flirting with the air. He's been the magic that makes every day an adventure and paints the world with vivid colour. I haven't even left yet but I already know that without Chances my life will be a grey and shadowy place. It'll be a half life.

"I'm sorry I couldn't stay and keep you safe," I whisper, putting my arms around his neck. "I wish we could ride away together and have adventures."

That's what would happen if life was like the tattered pony books I used to buy from charity shops, the ones written in the thirties where majors run pony clubs, children wear baggy breeches and the milkman's pony turns out to be a champion show jumper. Those stories were about as relevant to my life as books about the moon but I devoured them anyway. If my life was a pony story Chances and I could head into the woods and live happily ever after, or at least until the Major found us and told us we'd been picked for the Olympic team.

I laugh out loud at myself. I'm sixteen in a few weeks and I've been my mother's carer since I was twelve. Who knows better than me that real life doesn't work like this?

"Be good, boy," I say to Chances, kissing his soft nose. "I'll miss you so much."

I slide off the fence and haul my rucksack onto my shoulder. I call Scally, who's been chasing rabbits in the long grass, and together we walk through the farm gate and into the lane. I don't look back.

I daren't.

Hitchhiking in Bristol isn't difficult. There's a constant stream of traffic heading through the city, lorries trundle out to the motorways and tourists meander through in camper vans and people carriers. Usually I can find a lift to wherever I need to go and although I know it's taking a risk when you don't have any money, and the government doesn't think young carers deserve bus passes outside of school hours, you don't have much choice. Anyway, I've survived this long without bumping into an axe murderer.

But the one thing I haven't factored into my brilliant escape plan is that St Perran isn't exactly brimming with traffic. We might see one tractor an hour pass by the farm, but that's usually Harry anyway. The lane down to the village is probably really busy in the summer but in early November it's deserted. A pair of pheasants fly out of the hedge, squawking in outrage that I'm not a car to run them over, and a couple of farm vehicles rumble past but apart from that these it's very quiet. Even the village is empty. The lights are on the the grocer's shop and several cars crawl by but there aren't the lorries I'm hoping for. Truckers like company, it's boring driving hundreds of miles along the motorway, and they usually stop. I guess I just have to keep going.

I walk on through St Perran. Scally's getting tired so I carry her and my arms scream with the dead weight of dog. Just when I'm starting to lose hope a small van rounds the corner and slows down when I hold out my thumb.

An orange woman with a mane of blonde hair and glossy French manicured nails is at the wheel. She doesn't look like an axe murderer, unless axe murders are driving mobile beauty vans these days and chopping up their victims with emery boards.

"Where are you going, love?"

This is a good question. To be be honest I haven't really given it much thought. As far as my feet and the twenty quid in my pocket can take me, is the answer.

"Bristol?" I offer. It's as good as anywhere and at least I know a few people who might help. Lynn for one and, if I'm desperate, Dogood for another.

"I'm going to St Mellow to set up a bridal fayre," the driver says. "Is that any good?"

St Mellow is our nearest big town. I should be able to find a bus there or hitch another lift.

"That's brilliant, thanks!"

I hop in, Scally jumps onto my lap, and I pull the door shut. The van is warm and smells of perfume and nail varnish. The steering wheel is covered in pink fur, pink fluffy dice swing from the mirror while a collection of stuffed toys in lurid colours cower against the windscreen. It's nothing like Harry's truck where dried mud crusts the matts, sweet wrappers line the dash and the cab smells of wet dog.

I feel a sharp pang of loss.

The drive to the city passes in an awkward log jam of stop start conversation as the driver attempts to convince me I need a manicure and I do my best not to tell her anything about myself. She complains that Scally smells of dog (what else should she smell of?) and when she deposits us in the high street she looks thrilled to see the back of me. As she drives away I see her brushing Scally's hairs from the passenger seat and the windows are wide open.

Give me truckers any day. They don't give a monkey's about the state of my cuticles and they usually have lots of sweets too.

It's dark now. The lights are shining from shop doors and steamy windowed buses crammed with school children rumble by. I clip Scally's lead onto her collar and we wander the streets for a bit before heading to the coach station. The temperature has dropped a few degrees and it's raining too. I'm only wearing a hoody and I shiver. I daren't think of what it would be like back at the farm, the kettle whistling on the Aga, something delicious cooking in the oven, the horses pulling at their hay nets. No, if I let myself think about all this, I'll fall apart.

The shops close, the restaurants fill up and the rain grows heavier. Scally and I are both wet and shivering. I buy a cup of tea for me and a sausage roll to share but I daren't spend any more money. I only had twenty pounds to start with and I know that it won't last very long. The bus station is quiet and there's nothing due to leave for at least two more hours and even then I don't think I can afford it. I'll have to hitch again. Maybe if I walk to the big roundabout up by the supermarket I'll have a bit more luck?

I'm sitting on a bench, trying to figure out what to do next, when a man approaches. He's not much older than me, early twenties perhaps, but there's a sharpness in his face that's decades older. When he sits beside me I'm instantly I'm on full alert. The Shakespeare Estate is full of guys who look like this and they're never good news.

"Spare some change?"

I shoot him a sideways look. "I haven't got any."

"Don't give me that. Course you have. You're waiting for a bus. Must have some money. I'm asking nicely too."

Scally growls.

I stand up. "I don't have any. Sorry."

His hand grabs my elbow.

"Don't be like that, love. Just a quid or two."

"I said I haven't got anything!"

Scally barks and I try to pull my arm away but the stranger's grip is like iron.

"I'm asking nicely, *love*, but I won't be nice for long."

There's a hardness in his eyes that makes my stomach lurch. In the cold and darkness of a strange city and miles away from everyone I know, I'm suddenly afraid. An image of Chances in his stable, pulling at his hay and then charging to look over the door with ears pricked and nostrils flared, flickers through my mind and misery tightens. Was the wider world always this scary? Or have I felt safe for too long and forgotten? Have I forgotten how it really is?

I brace myself for the snatch at my rucksack that I know is coming next when there's a shout.

"Hey! Leave her alone!"

A lean figure steps out of the night and the sight of him is enough to send the stranger scuttling away into the shadows.

"You do like to live dangerously, Amber," says Drake Owen.

I can hardly believe it. "What are you doing here?"

"Looking for you, of course. Honestly, you do make life complicated. Have you any idea how hard it is to find somebody in a city this size and when it's dark?"

"How did you know where I was?"

Drake smiles. There are hollows under his eyes and lines I don't think where there before.

"It wasn't hard. Mrs. Pengelly in the village shop saw you getting into the *Paws and Claws* van. One phone call to them and bingo! I had the choice between the railway station and the coach station. It was hardly a case for CSI Cornwall."

For a minute I'm so pleased to see him that I can't stop smiling. Then I remember the events of the day and the smile withers on my lips.

"I'm surprised you're still talking to me. Hasn't Michael told you? I'm a drug addict and a bad influence on Emily. He's sacked Harry and given Kate her notice thanks to me. Watch out or you'll be next."

"I did hear something along those lines," Drake confesses.

"You ought to get away then. Don't let me stop you."

"Oh come on, Amber, don't be so ridiculous. You know I don't believe any of that stuff."

I stare at him. "Do I? How do I know, exactly? Through my psychic powers? It's not as though you came straight over to say you believed me, was it?"

Drake sinks onto the bench. He doesn't look at me. Instead he leans forward and strokes Scally.

"Sorry. I was busy quitting my job first."

"What?"

He straightens up. "You heard. Mike came charging into the yard in an absolute fury. He told me what happened and demanded that I had nothing more to do with you. When I said 'no' to him, he wasn't very pleased."

"You said 'no'?" I'm taken aback. "But why?"

"Because I know you wouldn't do anything like that!" Drake cries. "I trust you, Amber, and I believe in you. I've also known Emily long enough to be well aware just how jealous she is and how manipulative she can be. I told Michael that no yard was worth compromising my integrity for. That was when Harry arrived and we left to look for you. I should call him and let him know you're safe."

Harry and Drake have been searching for me together? Two guys who can't stand each other? Why would they do that?

"Because some things are more more important than feuds," Drake says simply when I ask this. "And Harry Crewe cares about you far more than he cares about continuing to blame me for the accident."

"I'm not coming back, Drake. I can't. I've caused too much damage. Everyone's better off without me. Michael won't give Harry his job back or let keep Kate the farm if they insist on helping me." I shake my head. "Just go back and forget about me. I'm not worth the trouble. Ask anyone."

Drake laughs.

"What? What's so funny?"

"You are," he says. "And you're totally, totally worth every second. Never doubt that! But you're so fiery and impulsive, Amber. Talk about making life difficult. If you'd stuck around rather than running away, you'd know every one's well aware by now that Emily's not as innocent as she makes out. And I mean *everyone*, Amber, including her father and the school. They all owe you a huge apology."

"What?"

He reaches out and takes my hands in his as though anchoring me.

"You gave Maddy your iPhone, didn't you? After Emily flushed hers away?"

I nod. "Yes, but I don't see what that's got to do with anything."

"You will when I tell you that Emily deliberately found Maddy to brag about what she did today. She didn't hold back either. She relished every detail and she had a lovely gloat about cutting stirrup leathers too."

"Sounds about right," I say glumly. "But it won't make any difference, Drake. Nobody will believe Maddy. She's just a little kid."

"Oh but they will and they already do," Drake says. "Maddy recorded every word on the iPhone you gave her. Then she went and played it to the Head teacher and then Kate who made sure Michael's listened as well. Nobody's in any doubt as to what happened and nobody thinks you're to blame. I promise."

My head is spinning.

"But Michael was so angry. He sacked Harry and he gave Kate her notice."

There's a grim expression on Drake's face. "He's mortified now, believe me. He's already apologised to Kate and I'm sure Harry will have his job back too. As for Emily, the last I heard before we left was that she's being sent to live with her mother so you won't have to put up with her again. It's lucky for Em that she only planted a small amount in your bag otherwise she'd be in huge trouble with the police for dealing."

This is too much to take in. "So everyone knows I'm innocent?"

"Yep," says Drake. 'It was a malicious trick designed to get you into trouble and out of the way. It almost worked too, didn't it?"

I stare at him.

"So it's all OK?" I can hardly believe it. "You've got your job back too?"

A frown crinkles Drake's forehead. "Well, that's a different issue. If Emily's no longer there to coach, I don't really have a job do I? I can't imagine Michael will want me hanging about costing him money." Then the frown lifts and he gives me a shy smile. "On the other hand, Emily not being around makes it a lot easier for us to go to the hunt ball together. If you still want to come with me, that is? And if you want to come back to St Perran?"

He's still holding my hands and I squeeze his fingers in answer.

"Yes," I say softly. "Yes, please."

And I'm answering both questions, which makes me feel all warm a funny inside.

Drake jumps to his feet and pulls me up with him.

"In that case," he says, twirling me round until the world is spinning. "Let's call Harry and take you home. Home where you belong, Amber. Home."

And this time there's absolutely no confusion because I know *exactly* where home is.

It's with Chances and the Crewes and all my friends at Perranview Farm.

EPILOGUE

Chances surges into an explosion of bucking across the paddock, kicking up his heels and tearing around in a blur of flame coloured coat. Treacle tries his hardest to keep up but his little legs are way to short and after a circuit or two he gives up and goes back to his grazing while Minty watches them both with a bemused expression.

"It's a lovely paddock," Harry says. "The orchard was getting really poached and it was never big enough anything bigger than a pony anyway."

Kate nods. "It's perfect for them, isn't it Amber?"

It certainly is. Chances and Treacle have moved into one of the paddocks at the Rectory and they look at home already. As I watch them grazing I think about how I used to ride Chances at night in this very place and it feels like another life. Now I can ride him every day and in the sand school too. It's like a dream come true.

"They seem very at home." Drake shields his eyes against the glare of the low winter sun. "It's a job well done."

"I think the least Michael could do was let Amber use the paddock," says Harry tightly. "He's lucky she didn't want to press charges against Emily."

The thought makes me shudder. To be honest, I want to put everything that happened behind me. I'm just enjoying going to school without having my life made a misery. Alan has certainly kicked butt somewhere because my teachers have finally moved me into proper sets and amazingly my science essay won a prize too. Maybe my dream of being a vet could still come true?

Wouldn't that be incredible?

"But Emily got off scot free," Harry is pointing out. "It doesn't seem fair."

"Hardly scot free," Kate says gently. "She's had to start a new boarding school and leave her father and home behind. Her mother's remarried and doesn't want her about and getting in the way. Emily's a damaged girl in her way, love. Money isn't everything."

"Hmmph," says Harry but I can tell he knows Kate's right. Isn't it ironic that Emily turned out to be just as troubled as any other teen? On the outside it looked like she had everything but she was so insecure and jealous that in reality she had nothing.

There's probably a lesson in that somewhere…

Anyway, in the two weeks since Emily's stunt so many things have happened and at such speed too that I can't quite believe it. The number one best thing of all has to be that my mum's wanted to visit me and is so much better that Dogood's been able to drive her down several times. Mum is still pale and quiet but she's lost the pinched and inwards look she's had for so long and she loves chatting to Kate, walking in the fresh air and and getting to know Chances. I don't know what the future hold for her and I know she'll be in treatment for some time yet, maybe even for years, but I feel happy knowing she's safe and having all the help she needs. I tried my very best to look after her but I realise now that Dogood was right all along; I couldn't look after Mum on my own. Not when she was so ill and needed specialist help. I'll be staying here with Kate, there's no more talk of hostels, and maybe in the future Mum could come and live in St Perran too? The place worked its magic on me so why not on her?

I'm so excited by this thought. These days everything feels possible. It's amazing.

"Penny for them?" Harry says.

"I was just thinking how much has happened," I reply and he nods.

"It's incredible, isn't it? Michael offering you the use of the paddock and giving Mum the job as his full time house keeper as well as saying the farm lease is ours for as long as we ever want it." He gives me his cheeky grin. "It's almost as though he feels guilty about something and wants to make amends!"

I laugh. "Now whatever gave you that idea?"

"Chances looks very settled," Drake observes. Turning to Harry he adds, "And talking of being settled, Harry, I've a proposition for you if you're willing to hear me out?"

Harry shrugs one shoulder. He's still not Drake's biggest fan but since they managed to survive their trip to find me without killing one another there's been an uneasy truce.

"Of course he'll listen." Kate lays a hand on her son's shoulder. "It's time we put the past behind us. What happened to Ben was awful but it was an accident and I know the last thing he would want is to let it damage us any more. My husband was always such a positive person and he saw the good in people. Like you, Harry my love."

Harry nods quietly and I know Kate's right. I never knew his father but Harry saw the good in me when nobody else did and he saw the good in Chances too.

"I'm not going to stay here forever," Drake says, sweeping his arm in the direction of the Rectory. "There's no future here but I would like to think that there could still be one for me in St Perran. Harry, you've got land, you've got barns and you've got a long term lease now. How about you and I go into partnership and run an eventing and schooling business from this farm? We could build it up over time?"

Harry is wide-eyed. "Are you serious?"

"I've never been more so in my life," Drake says. "It'll be hard work but I think it could be a success, I really do. I want to train Amber too and I know the talent scouts are already impressed with her. She's got a great future ahead. There are no guarantees, of course, but I think we could have something really special here. You could even go back to college part time if I shoulder the majority of the running. I'm not wealthy but I do have some savings and I'd be more than willing to put them into a business with you and find a new sponsor. What do you say?"

These two guys have been enemies and rivals for years but they've already come together once to help me. As Harry considers the proposal I find I'm holding my breath and hoping with everything in me that they can do so again.

For a moment Harry hesitates. Then the corners of his mouth curl upwards in exact time with the rising of my heart. Slowly, he holds his hand out to Drake.

"Why not?" Harry says and they shake hands. Then he catches my eye and smiles, a secret smile that's just for me. "There are some chances worth taking and some people definitely worth taking them for."

In the paddock Chances crops the grass, tail floating in the breeze like a banner and his chestnut coat gleaming in the winter sunshine.

My horse. My world. My dream come true.

He's mine.

We're safe and we've finally come home.

THE END

ABOUT THE AUTHOR

Ruth Saberton is the bestselling author of *Katy Carter Wants a Hero* and *Escape for the Summer*. She also writes upmarket commercial fiction under the pen names Jessica Fox, Georgie Carter and Holly Cavendish.

Born in London, Ruth now lives in beautiful Cornwall. She has travelled to many places and recently returned from living in the Caribbean but nothing compares to the rugged beauty of the Cornish coast. Ruth loves to chat with readers so please do add her as a Facebook friend and follow her on Twitter.

Twitter: @ruthsaberton
Facebook: Ruth Saberton
www.ruthsaberton.com

Printed in Great Britain
by Amazon

37670049R00092